16 6/14 7/16
16 X 6/14 v 1/18

W9-CEL-951

The
BLACK
HEART
CRYPT

THE HAUNTED MYSTERY SERIES
BY CHRIS GRABENSTEIN

The Crossroads
Winner of the Agatha Award and the Anthony Award

The Hanging Hill
Winner of the Agatha Award

The Smoky Corridor

The Black Heart Crypt

~ A ~
HAUNTED MYSTERY

THE BLACK HEART CRYPT

CHRIS GRABENSTEIN

Random House 🏠 New York

Text copyright © 2011 by Chris Grabenstein
Jacket art copyright © 2011 by Scott Altmann

All rights reserved. Published in the United States by Random House Children's Books, a division of Random House, Inc., New York.

Random House and the colophon are registered trademarks of Random House, Inc.

Visit us on the Web! www.randomhouse.com/kids

Educators and librarians, for a variety of teaching tools, visit us at www.randomhouse.com/teachers

ChrisGrabenstein.com

Library of Congress Cataloging-in-Publication Data
Grabenstein, Chris.
The black heart crypt / Chris Grabenstein. — 1st ed.
p. cm. — (The haunted mystery series ; bk. 4)
Summary: A 200-year-old ghost inhabits a living ancestor in order to take revenge on eleven-year-old Zack and his family.
ISBN 978-0-375-86900-6 (trade) — ISBN 978-0-375-96900-3 (lib. bdg.)
ISBN 978-0-375-89987-4 (ebook)
[1. Ghosts—Fiction. 2. Demonology—Fiction. 3. Revenge—Fiction.] I. Title.
PZ7.G7487 Bl 2011 [Fic]—dc22 2011001939

Printed in the United States of America

10 9 8 7 6 5 4 3 2 1

First Edition

for J. J. Myers,
who is the love of my life and,
hopefully, my afterlife

1

Zack Jennings did not want to chase a slobbering black dog with glowing red eyeballs up into the Haddam Hill Cemetery three nights before Halloween.

It was Zipper's idea.

They were in the backyard after dinner, playing with a squishy yellow ball, when Zipper picked up the other dog's scent and went tearing down the highway after it.

"Zipper? Halt! Stay! Come!"

Zack wasn't exactly sure which command to use to stop his dog from chasing after the thundering black beast, which had to be some kind of hellhound; otherwise its eyes wouldn't be a pair of red-hot coals.

But Zipper did not halt, stay, or come. The small dog slipped through the cemetery's wrought-iron railings to pursue the monster, which had so many rippling muscles Zack figured it must belong to the Gym for Gigantic Dogs.

Of course he couldn't squeeze between the railings like Zipper had, and he wasn't much at scaling fences, especially when his glasses got all foggy, so he dashed around to the back of the cemetery, where he knew there was a gate because one night, back in June, he and his friend Davy had hidden in this very same cemetery to escape a knife-wielding nut job whose body was being controlled by an evil ancestor.

A *dead* evil ancestor.

Yep. Ghosts can do that. They can slip their souls into the bodies of family members and totally take them over.

Zack yanked open the gate and shuffled through the sea of leaves smothering the ground between tombstones. A chilly autumn nip was in the air. The moon was hidden behind a pile of angry dark clouds. The sky was a murky black. Three nights before Halloween, this cemetery was creepier than ever.

"Zipper?" Zack's voice echoed off a marble monument. "Where are you, boy?"

Finally, his dog barked a quick volley of yaps to let Zack know he was extremely busy.

Then Zack heard a deep, throaty rumble. The demon dog!

"Hang on, Zip! I'm coming!"

Zack swung around a concrete angel and raced over to a tomb the size of a small cabin—the biggest, darkest mausoleum in the whole Haddam Hill Cemetery. Its arched wooden doorway was sealed tight with a black heart-shaped lock. Even in the gloom of night, Zack could read the name carved into the stone slab over the entryway:

"Zipper?" No answer.

Zack trotted around the stone building, which sort of looked like a miniature church made out of gray Lego blocks.

"Zipper?"

He heard a weird whimper that sounded like a weary sheep bleat.

"Zip?"

His dog came padding around the corner of the blockhouse with a bewildered grin on his snout.

"The big black dog disappeared on you, didn't he, boy?"

Zipper wagged his tail excitedly, as if to say, *Yeah, yeah. It was freaky.*

Zack bent down to rub his buddy's head.

"Well, maybe next time you'll listen to me when I tell you not to chase after devil dogs."

Zipper leapt up to lick Zack's face. Zack laughed.

That is, he laughed until he heard the sharp slice of a shovel blade digging into dirt.

Someone else was in the cemetery.

Zipper hunkered down on the ground in pounce mode.

Zack pressed his back against the Ickleby family crypt in an attempt to disappear into the shadows.

Sticky cobwebs attacked the back of his head, making him feel like he'd just brushed up against a giant wad of cotton candy. Peeling away the gooey strands, Zack peered over at a cluster of grime-streaked headstones, where he saw a burly man with a bushy beard, who was dressed in coveralls, sinking his shovel blade into the ground, digging up rocky clumps of dirt. A softly glowing lantern propped atop a nearby headstone projected his hulking shadow up into the tangled tree branches, where it loomed like a floating ogre.

Fortunately, the guy wasn't a ghost. Zack could tell. Ever since he'd moved to Connecticut from New York City with his dad and stepmom, he'd learned a whole bunch of junk about the spirit world—what ghosts can do and what they can't. He probably knew more than any eleven-year-old should legally be allowed to.

For instance, he knew that a ghost could take over the body of its blood relative, but unless it did that, it couldn't do much besides wail and moan and try to scare you into hurting yourself.

A ghost couldn't hold a shovel, and in Zack's experience, digging a hole in the ground by lantern light wasn't exactly something an evil spirit took over a relative's body to do. He felt pretty confident that the dude digging the hole wasn't a ghost or a possessed person.

The man started singing as he dug, a tune Zack recognized from recess on the playground:

"Don't ever laugh when a hearse goes by,
For you may be the next to die."

Zack looked at Zipper and put a finger to his lips. They would try to tiptoe out of the graveyard without being seen or heard.

"The worms crawl in, the worms crawl out,
The worms play pinochle on your snout."

Zack and Zipper crept closer to the gate. The man kept digging, kept up his steady *stomp-slice-shook-flump, stomp-slice-shook-flump.*

"There's one little worm that's very shy,
  Crawls in your stomach and out your eye."

Zack and Zipper made it to the graveyard gate.

The digging stopped.

"Isn't that right, boy?"

Okay. Zack didn't remember those lyrics. He pushed open the squeaky gate.

"Freeze!" the gravedigger shouted.

Zack froze.

And this time, Zipper obeyed, too!

3

Somewhere in the distance, Zack heard a stray cat meowing at the moon.

Then he heard boots clomping up behind him.

"I heard you callin' to your dog, boy," said the man, who kept coming closer. "Zipper. What kind of name is that for a dog?"

Slowly, Zack turned around.

The man was standing six feet behind him, holding his clay-draggled shovel like a knight's lance with one hand, the flickering lantern with the other.

"Well," said Zack, wishing his throat weren't so dry, "Zipper is very fast and . . ."

"Dogs ought to be named Fido, Duke, Sparky. What you two doin' here, anyway? Cemetery's closed."

"Um," said Zack, "Zipper chased a cat up the hill from the highway."

"A cat?" The creepy gravedigger raised the lantern up beside his craggy face. "You sure it weren't a dog? A big black dog?"

Zack gulped. "Pardon?"

The gravedigger bugged out his eyes. "A big black dog with fiery-red eyeballs. What some folks call a Black Shuck, a ghostly black beast what guards graveyards from foul spirits." The man grinned menacingly. "Wonder why he let you two in."

"It was just a cat," said Zack.

The stray cat yowled again. With its strangled cry, it sounded like a baby screaming for its bottle.

"Well, we better get going."

"Yep. You should. Ain't very wise to be in a boneyard this close to Halloween unless, of course, you've got some serious business to attend to, such as digging a new grave."

Zack was scared but also confused, so he said, "Huh?"

The gravedigger nodded toward the hole he'd been scooping out. "Mr. Henry H. Heckman has arrived just in time for Halloween, when he'll crawl up out of the ground to go take care of whatever business he left undone when he died."

"Heckman?"

"That's what I said, boy. Putting him in the family plot. There's all sorts of Heckmans buried up here on Haddam Hill."

Yeah, Zack wanted to say. He had met one of them back in June: a dead bus driver named Bud Heckman.

"Yep," the gravedigger went on, "Heckmans have lived and died in these parts since before the Revolutionary War."

8

"Just like the Icklebys, huh?"

The gravedigger lost his sly smile. "Icklebys ain't from around here, boy."

"Really? I saw their name on that big tomb over there, so I figured . . ."

"Icklebys don't belong here and neither do you two! Git!"

Zipper snarled.

The gravedigger raised his shovel. "Git!"

"We're 'gitting,'" said Zack.

"Good! And don't never come back here no more!"

"Don't worry," said Zack. "We won't."

Because a graveyard was the last place Zack Jennings wanted to be this close to Halloween.

Too many worm-eaten ghosts with pinochle cards up their snouts.

Thirteen demons stared at the gravedigger through the cold stone walls of the Ickleby crypt.

"Let us out!" screamed the youngest soul trapped inside. "Let us out, you grody gravedigger, or I'll ice you, man!"

His elders shook their heads. They knew that all the gravedigger would hear of the young man's rant was the howl of a distant wind.

"Quiet, boy," rasped Barnabas, the family patriarch and the oldest Ickleby entombed on Haddam Hill. "The gravedigger cannot hear you."

"I don't care, man. Someday, I'm gonna bust down these walls and break outta here!"

"Ah, you're all wet, ya sap," said the ghost of Crazy Izzy Ickleby, a gangster who had made his fortune running rum with Al Capone during Prohibition. "Besides, it ain't the stones locking us in."

"It is the spell," said Barnabas. "The cursed spell!"

Barnabas, who had died in 1749 and, even as a ghost, still wore his bandit mask and tricornered hat, kept an eye on their unexpected visitor, the young boy in the glasses, as he disappeared down the hill with his dog.

"That child." His voice was the husky croak of a strangled crow.

"What about him?" snapped the tough-talking gangster.

"When he leaned up against the wall, I felt a most peculiar chill. He is a Jennings."

The twelve other demons hissed when he said the name.

The Icklebys hated the Jenningses.

They had hated them ever since the day thirty years ago when certain members of the Jennings clan had confined these thirteen Ickleby souls to this cramped crypt.

"We shall have our revenge on that boy," said Barnabas. "And soon. Very soon."

"They're not out there, George," said Judy.

"You're sure?"

Zack's dad and stepmother were standing in the kitchen, looking out through the big bay window into the backyard.

"Come on," said George. "Zack and Zip might be in trouble."

"Or they might just be in the *front* yard," said Judy.

"Halloween's coming."

"So?"

"The veil grows thin!"

Judy shook her head to clear out her ears. "What?"

"Halloween. The veil between the worlds of the living and the dead is thinnest on October thirty-first!"

Oh, boy, thought Judy.

Ever since George had learned that Zack could see ghosts (the same way George had been able to when he was a boy), he had been spending a little too much time on his daily commute to and from New York City reading books about the spirit world.

George grabbed a flashlight. He and Judy hurried out the back door.

"What's that?" George swung his beam across the yard, pausing at a half-buried lump in the grass. "It looks like a head. A shrunken head!"

"That's Zipper's ball," Judy said calmly.

"Are you sure? Maybe a ghost shrunk Zack's head."

"That's not Zack, sweetheart. His head isn't yellow and squishy."

George tilted up his flashlight and moved the beacon across a flurry of swaying branches.

"There's a ghost up there, waving at us! See him?"

"That's a tree, hon."

"You sure?"

"Ghosts don't have that many limbs. Or bird nests."

"But trees can have ghosts hidden inside them. Zack told me about the tree that crashed into the backyard, how the ghost trapped inside broke free and went on an all-out evil spree."

Judy took George's arm and cuddled up against him. "That ghost is all gone."

"I know. But maybe he'll come back."

"I don't think he can."

"On Halloween, anything is possible. They all get a hall pass on Halloween."

Judy smiled.

George kept on going. "Communicating with ancestors and departed loved ones is easiest near Halloween, the night when souls once again journey through this world on their way to the Summerlands, which is what ancient Druids called the afterlife."

"George?"

"Yeah?"

"You ever think about going back to reading mysteries and military histories?"

"Why? Do you think I'm going overboard with this stuff?"

"Maybe. A little. Kind of."

"I'm just trying to make sure Zack is safe. Halloween isn't easy for a guy who sees ghosts, trust me."

"Look, I'm sure if Zack sees anything paranormal, he'll tell us."

"I hope so. Maybe he should wear a disguise so the wandering spirits don't wreak revenge on him."

"Why would they do that?"

"I don't know. They're dead. They're not thinking straight."

Judy heard leaves crunching.

"What's that?" George swung his flashlight toward the forest.

And practically blinded his son.

"Hey, Dad. Hey, Mom." Zack had to shield his eyes with his forearm. Zipper stood at his side, merrily wagging his tail.

"Are you two okay?" his father asked.

"Yeah. Zipper went chasing after a devil dog."

"A what?" said Judy.

"A big black dog with glowing red eyeballs. He chased it all the way up to the Haddam Hill Cemetery."

"Ah," said his father. "A Black Shuck! They guard graveyards. I read about those."

"You're sure you're okay?" asked Judy.

"Yeah. The dog-beast vanished."

His father nodded knowingly. "They'll do that."

"But," said Zack, "we might want to keep an eye out for Henry H. Heckman."

"The baker on Main Street?" said George, who had grown up in North Chester and knew everybody in town.

"Yeah. He just died. The gravedigger figures he'll be up and walking around on Monday night, seeing how it's Halloween and all." Zack yawned. "I'm pooped. Think I'll head up to bed."

"You still want to go pumpkin picking tomorrow?" his father asked, his brow wrinkled with concern.

"Yeah. And Malik and Azalea are really looking forward to it, too."

"Great," said Judy, smiling warmly. "Good night, hon. Don't forget to brush your teeth."

"I won't. Come on, Zip."

The two of them headed into the house.

"Okay," said George, "that does it. We're going to need reinforcements. I'm texting Aunt Ginny."

Judy, who had only married George five months earlier, was still a little foggy about his family. "Which one is she?"

"Virginia. The youngest of my father's three sisters. She helped me when I was Zack's age and could see ghosts."

"Really? How?"

"She made them go away."

Near midnight, a young woman, maybe twenty-four, scaled the cemetery fence and approached the Ickleby crypt.

"Hey," said the youngest soul trapped inside, the one the others called Eddie Boy, the Ickleby who had been gunned down by the Massachusetts State Police during a convenience store robbery gone bad in 1979. "Who's this chick? She is loo-king goooood!"

The girl had ringlets of wild blond hair curlicuing out from under the peak of her hooded cape. Her cloak was made of black velvet and lined with deep-purple silk. A pentagram pendant, a five-pointed sterling silver star, dangled on a chain around her neck.

"She," said Barnabas, his voice a sinister squawk, "is one who can be of much use to us. Her name . . ."

He strained to suck thoughts from the young woman's mind. Having been a ghost for over 260 years, Barnabas Ickleby had honed telepathic powers few other spirits possessed.

". . . is Jenny Ballard, and, children, it seems she fancies herself a witch. She longs to fill her mind with evil thoughts. Miss Ballard should prove quite receptive to all my subconscious suggestions!"

The other twelve souls sniggered at the remark.

"I shall infest her mind with wickedness!" Barnabas gloated. "And then—I shall send her forth to seek out our new earthen vessel!"

fast asleep in his bedroom, Zack sure hoped he was dreaming.

If not, all sorts of dead people were dropping by to wish him a happy Halloween.

First to arrive was Rodman Willoughby, the dead chauffeur for the Spratlings, the family that used to be the richest one in all of North Chester because they owned the famous Spratling Clockworks Factory.

Seeing Mr. Willoughby sitting on the edge of the bed in his black suit and driver's cap wasn't too big of a shock because Zack had already seen Mr. Willoughby's ghost at school, a couple of days after the old guy had died.

"On Halloween," Mr. Willoughby whispered mysteriously, "I must hurry home to take care of the Cadillac. It needs its oil changed."

That was why Zack figured this had to be a dream. In his experience, dead people never had to whisper, because nobody could hear them except the people they wanted to hear them, anyway. Whispering was a total waste of time for ghosts.

Before Zack could say, "Thanks for popping by," Mr. Willoughby turned into Davy Wilcox—a ten-year-old farm boy in denim overalls with a slingshot sticking out of his back pocket. Weird junk like old men turning into ten-year-old boys happened only in dreams. Or movies.

"Howdy, pardner," said dream Davy.

Zack tried to say, "Hey," back, but since he was asleep, he couldn't make his mouth move.

"Best be prepared come Halloween," said Davy. "Whole mess of ghosts will come a'swarmin' up out of the ground. It's the dadgum spooks' and spirits' big night out on the town."

Davy disappeared and became the ghost of Kathleen Williams, a dead nightclub singer and star of Broadway musicals back in the 1950s. Dressed in a black-and-orange sequined gown, she sat with her legs crossed on the edge of the bed and held a microphone in her hand. The black widow spider ring on her finger looked like it was alive!

"Hiya, Zack!" She turned to an unseen accompanist: "Hit it, Joe!"

Now Zack heard heavy pipe organ music as Kathleen Williams started belting out a little-known verse from "The Hearse Song":

"Your stomach turns a slimy green
And pus pours out like whipping cream.
You spread it on a slice of bread
And that's what you eat when you are dead."

Zack was about to laugh at the gross lyrics, but in a flash, his dream became a nightmare.

8

Kathleen Williams turned into Susan Potter Jennings.

Zack's dead mother.

The way she'd looked right before she died. Shrunken and shriveled. Tufts of hair sprouting out on top of her vein-riddled head. A surgeon's scar rippling down her throat until it disappeared beneath the collar of her hospital gown, the gown she had died in after wasting away to little more than ninety pounds, her whole body wracked by the poisonous drugs meant to kill her cancer.

You did this to me, Zack remembered his mother wheezing at him as she was dying. *You ruined my life.*

In his head, Zack now knew that what his mother had said wasn't true. But sometimes, when it was dark and he was alone, Zack wondered if he had somehow magically killed Susan Potter Jennings so he could get a do-over, a happy new life with a mom who actually loved him. His stepmother. Judy Magruder Jennings.

Now Zack could hear wet mucus rumbling around

inside his dead mother's leathery lungs. Her eyes went wide, frantically searching the room.

"Zachary?" she moaned from the foot of the bed. "Zachary?"

She stretched out her skeletal arms as if to hug him, something Zack couldn't remember her ever doing while she was alive.

"Where are you?"

Zack tried to shut his eyes even tighter, but he couldn't make the ghostly apparition disappear, because his dead mother wasn't there as a ghost—she was trapped inside a dream.

"Zachary!"

Uh-oh.

Zack's dead mother only called him Zachary when she was totally mad at him—like when he embarrassed her in front of her rich girlfriends or made up a stupid story or played with his action figures, which she called his dollies.

Okay, she had pretty much called Zack Zachary every minute of every day for the first nine years of his life.

But this "Zachary" sounded, well, different. Not angry but scared. Terrified.

Even though Zack could see her, could feel the weight of her emaciated body on his bed, *she* couldn't see *him*. She kept clawing at the air with hands as gnarled as eagle talons.

"I will come," she said, her voice weak and thin. "I will come for you, Zachary!"

No thanks, Zack wanted to say. *Stay in hell or purgatory or limbo or wherever they've got your soul locked up these days.*

But he couldn't say anything.

It was still a dream. The worst dream he'd ever had in his whole life.

"Wake up, Zack," said a new voice. A man's. His tone firm and gentle. "Wake up, champ."

Zack pried open an eye.

The only creature on the edge of his bed was Zipper, who was snoring and kicking his hind legs probably because his dreams involved chasing squirrels.

Zack sat up. Felt his dog's very real, very warm fur. Okay. Zack was definitely awake.

"We'll get through this thing," said the unseen man. "We'll do it together."

Zack looked toward his homework desk and saw an athletic man with a shock of white hair. The man was wearing a familiar sheriff's uniform.

"You better go back to sleep, champ. Trust me—you'll need your strength when my sisters show up."

"Grandpa Jim?"

The old man winked.

Then he disappeared.

Zack's grandpa Jim had died three years earlier, just before Zack's real mother passed away.

Grandpa Jim wasn't part of the dream.

Grandpa Jim was a ghost.

The young woman in the hooded cape stood transfixed, staring up at the name engraved above the entrance to the crypt.

ICKLEBY

Jenny Ballard was hanging out in yet another grave-yard at midnight because she had decided she was tired of being a waitress at the Bob's Big Boy out near the interstate.

She wanted to become a witch.

And not the airy-fairy, goody-goody kind that floated around in bubbles. She wanted to be a bad witch, the old-fashioned wicked kind from fairy tales. She wanted to cast evil spells on all the popular girls who had made fun of her when she wore her retainer to middle school. She wanted to turn all the bad tippers at Bob's Big Boy into toads.

She fluffed out her corkscrewy hair and moved one step closer to the massive mausoleum.

She felt a deep chill. Goose pimples popped up on the soft undersides of her pale arms.

"Jenny!"

There was no one else in the graveyard, yet she clearly heard a man with a scratchy voice whispering her name.

"Jenny!"

Her breathing came faster.

"He is one of us," the ominous voice continued. *"Bring him here on Halloween. Reap your reward!"*

Jenny had no idea who or what the voice was talking about or why she was hearing it.

"Bring him unto us, Jenny, on All Hallows' Eve."

Okay. The invisible dude with the monster-movie voice had to be some kind of ancient, disembodied soul. Who else would call Halloween by its old-school name: All Hallows' Eve?

"I will bring him," Jenny mumbled.

She decided to ask for more information.

"Who is it that thou seek?"

But the bird voice was gone.

In its place, all she heard was the thick fluttering of wings.

She looked up. An inky black raven sat perched atop the head of an angel statue at the peak of the tomb's steeply slanted roof. The bird glared down at Jenny with glowing black eyes.

"Haw!" it croaked.

Jenny bent into a slight bow. "Yes. Of course."

The bird was right. It was time for her leave.

Time for her to go find the man the evil voice in her head said it needed so desperately.

10

Virginia "Ginny" Jennings and her two sisters, Hannah and Sophie, were eating breakfast poolside at their condo complex in Boca Raton, Florida.

Ginny had brought along Pyewacket, her white-and-gray cat, who sat purring contentedly in her lap.

Breakfast for Ginny was a banana and an English muffin. Her sister Hannah was mixing fiber powder in a glass of prune juice, while Sophie had a gooey cheese Danish, a package of little powdered doughnuts, and a foil-wrapped pair of Pop-Tarts.

It was early morning, but the sun, blindingly bright and glimmering off the pool, had already baked the southern tip of Florida to a muggy eighty-six degrees, which was why Ginny always wore flowery Hawaiian muumuus—loose-fitting dresses with ample armpit room for breezy ventilation.

Hannah, on the other hand, wore prim blouses (with the collar buttoned) under cardigan sweaters, while Sophie, who was rather plump, came down to the pool each morning decked out in polka dots, which made her look like a bouquet of balloons.

A young man shoved a wheelchair up to the table next to the sisters'.

"Wait here while I get your food, Uncle Gus," he said to the shrunken man sitting in it, who was wearing a flimsy flannel bathrobe.

"Eh?" The old man brought a trembling hand up to his hairy ear.

"I SAID WAIT HERE!" Then he added under his breath, "You deaf old fart."

Ginny gasped.

The horrible nephew whirled around to face her.

"Mind your business, you old hag."

He stomped away.

Pyewacket the cat hissed at his back—three times.

"Sisters," said Ginny, "I believe the brinded cat hath hissed thrice."

"Virginia?" said Hannah, quite sternly. "We are retired. How many times must I remind you?"

"But . . ."

"Re-tired. To this, we three did agree, did we not?"

"Oh, yes," said Sophie, a blizzard of white powdered doughnut sugar showering down on her ample bosom. "We did. I remember. We agreed."

Ginny sighed.

"Of course, Hannah," she said. "You are correct. We are retired."

* * *

Birds chirped. Uncle Gus wheezed in the wheelchair. Hannah snapped open her very organized plastic pillbox and prepared to pop her daily regimen of anti-everything medication. Sophie nibbled a chocolate-frosted Pop-Tart. Ginny peeled open her banana and sipped ice water through a straw.

"Oh, I almost forgot," said Ginny. "You'll never guess who I exchanged text messages with last week."

"Text messages?" said Hannah. "What on earth are those?"

"Why, I suppose you could say they are postcards you can read on your telephone."

"How?" inquired Hannah, tossing her head back to swallow her pills the way a pelican swallows a fish.

"You read the message on the screen."

"I don't really like telephones," said Sophie with a quivering giggle. "They're a bit like children, aren't they? Always making noise, always insisting that you answer them *immediately*."

The comment saddened Ginny. She and her sisters had never married, never had children. All three were what were once called spinsters.

That was why all three had always doted on their only nephew, Georgie, the son of their brother, James. Of course, Georgie was all grown up now, a very important lawyer in New York City, living in North Chester, Connecticut, the Jennings family's ancestral home.

Georgie even had a son of his own, a boy named

Zachary, whom the aunts had not spent much time with, because his mother, a rather dour woman named Susan, had made it frightfully clear that her husband's aged aunts were not welcome in the young family's swanky New York City apartment.

The three sisters had, however, returned to New York after Susan's untimely death and, more happily, eighteen months later, for George's second wedding, when he married the lovely and talented Judy Magruder.

Ginny pulled a sleek cell phone out of her purse, swiped her fingers across its glass face, turning it on, and set it down on the table.

A faint smile creased Hannah's sour lips. "So, tell us, Virginia: How is Georgie?"

"How's Zack?" asked Sophie, her eyes sparkling like sugared plums. "And Judy? I liked Judy."

"They're all fine," said Ginny.

Suddenly, her cell phone started vibrating.

"Oh, my!" gasped Sophie, fanning her hands, making her upper arms jiggle. "It's alive!"

"No, Sophie," said Ginny. "That simply means I have received a new text message."

She glanced at the screen.

"Oh, dear. I should have turned my phone on earlier! We must fly home to North Chester. Immediately. Georgie needs us!"

"*fly home*, Virginia?" said Hannah. "Whatever is the problem?"

"It's Zachary," said Ginny, quickly looking around to make certain no one was eavesdropping. "Georgie's son has—*the gift*."

"Oh, dear," said Hannah.

"Oh me, oh my," added Sophie, nervously nibbling the sprinkled edge of her second Pop-Tart.

Ginny was about to give them more details when the boorish nephew returned with a sloppy bowl of mush, which he slammed down so hard in front of his wheelchair-bound uncle, chunky gray clumps leapt up and splattered his bathrobe.

"Hah! Look at you, sitting in your high chair, food all over your face. No wonder you need diapers! You're a big baby!"

Ginny had seen enough.

She placed her banana peel on the table and plucked the plastic straw out of her water glass.

"Sisters?" she said, angrily arching an eyebrow.

"We three agree," said Hannah and Sophie.

Ginny held up the straw as if it were a conductor's baton she meant to fling at the oafish young man.

But she didn't.

Because at that very instant, the baboon seemed to slip on something very slick, very wet.

Why, it was almost as if he had stepped on a banana peel.

He lost his footing and, arms whirling, fell into the swimming pool.

Ginny smiled.

So did her two sisters.

So did Uncle Gus in the wheelchair.

"I believe our work here is done," said Ginny, plopping the plastic straw back into her water glass. "Shall we go upstairs and pack?"

"Oh, yes," said Sophie.

"Indeed," added Hannah.

The three sisters walked over to the elderly man left stranded in his wheelchair.

"Would you like us to take you up to your room, Augustus?" offered Hannah.

"Thank you. How very kind of you."

Then the three Jennings sisters, with Hannah piloting the wheelchair, left the poolside patio, ignoring the frantic pleas of the young brute flailing about in the water so violently, he would probably slosh it all out before he remembered he knew how to swim.

12

Early Saturday, two days before Halloween, Zack; his stepmom, Judy; and his two best friends from school, Malik Sherman and Azalea Torres, piled into Judy's car and headed out to pick pumpkins at Paproski's Pumpkin Patch, a farm a few miles south of North Chester.

They took Zipper, too, because pumpkin picking was an outdoor activity. But Zack would need to make sure that Zip didn't pee on somebody else's just-picked pumpkin.

Zack's father would've joined them for pumpkin picking, but even though it was Saturday, he was extremely busy managing the affairs of the Pettimore Charitable Trust, which, thanks to Zack and Malik, had just inherited a ton of gold. Literally. The boys had found more than two thousand pounds of solid gold bars hidden underneath their middle school.

Malik and a school janitor named Wade Muggins, who kind of sort of accidentally helped discover the gold, were supposed to receive big rewards. Malik would use his share to help his mother pay her colossal medical bills. Mr.

Muggins would probably use his to buy an electric guitar and several cowbells.

"Here we go, guys," said Judy as the car bumped down a gravel road toward the field where pumpkin pickers parked. Zack could see acres of wilted greenery spotted with bright orange balls. Hay bales, some with comical scarecrows squatting on top, lined paths to wagon rides, an apple cider stand, and a corn maze—what Paproski's Pumpkin Patch called the Amazing Haunted Maize Maze.

"Did you know that the tradition of carving gourds into lanterns dates back thousands of years to Africa?" said Malik, who was African American and quite proud of his heritage. He was also the smartest kid in Zack's sixth-grade class.

"So why do they call them Jack O'Lanterns?" asked Azalea, who had stopped doing her total Goth look but had maintained much of her Goth 'tude. "Were Jack and the beanstalk from Africa, too?"

"Doubtful," said Malik. "The term 'jack-o'-lantern' comes from the phenomenon of strange lights flickering over the Irish peat bogs, called ignis fatuus or jack-o'-lantem."

"Irish, huh?" said Azalea. "No wonder his last name is O'Lantern."

"Indeed," said Malik, who sometimes talked like a walking Wikipedia. "Throughout Ireland and Britain, there is a long tradition of carving lanterns from vegetables. Particularly the turnip and mangel-wurzel."

Behind the wheel, Judy laughed. "The mangel-what?"

"The mangel-wurzel," said Malik. "It is a little-known root vegetable hailing from the same family as beets."

"You mean the yucky family?" said Azalea, scrunching up her nose. "I hate beets!"

"Me too," said Judy. "They smell like dirt."

"Exactly!" said Azalea.

Zack, who was riding up front in the passenger seat, smiled. It was so cool to have a carful of friends, not to mention one totally awesome stepmother. It sort of made up for the first nine years of his life, when he had no friends and a mother who never smiled.

"I heard this legend about a guy named Stingy Jack," said Zack, turning around in his seat.

"Aw, you're not that stingy, Zack," said Azalea, winking at Malik, who chuckled.

"*Jack*, not Zack!"

"Whatever."

"When Stingy Jack died, the devil couldn't take his soul, on account of some trick Jack played on the devil when he was still alive. And God wouldn't let Stingy Jack into heaven, either, because Jack had hung out with the devil while he was living. So after he died, they both tossed Jack out and he became this doomed soul, wandering around with nothing but a glowing coal to light his way. Jack put the coal into a carved-out turnip and he's been roaming around ever since. The Irish people called his ghost Jack of the Lantern, which, you know, became jack-o'-lantern."

"This Jack ghost," said Azalea, "you ever meet him, Zack?"

"Nope."

"How about you, Mrs. Jennings?"

"Can't say I've had the pleasure," said Judy, turning to park where a guy flapping a flag directed her.

"They say people carve pumpkins and turn them into lanterns to scare off Jack and all the other spirits roaming around on Halloween night," said Zack.

"How about that dude?" said Azalea, gesturing at the flag waver, who was costumed in a bedsheet and skeleton mask. "Is he a ghost?"

"No," said Malik. "Otherwise, we wouldn't be able to see him."

"But Zack and Mrs. Jennings could, right?" said Azalea. She'd missed a lot of what had happened when Zack and Malik were dealing with the roaming spirits underneath their middle school, because, well, Azalea's body (and brain) had been taken over by an evil ancestor.

Fortunately, Azalea's possession had lasted less than a day. When the evil spirit left her, her memories of the event said buh-bye, too, which was weird because Azalea usually had a photographic memory. She didn't have to cram for exams; she had all the textbook pages burned into her brain cells.

So of course Azalea remembered the time when Zack told her that he could see ghosts.

His stepmom, Judy, had the gift, too. His dad used to

have it but lost it when he turned thirteen. The gift had returned, however, when he really, really needed it: when Zack was being chased through a maze of tunnels by a brains-gobbling zombie.

Of course, his dad might have relost his ghost-seeing ability just as quickly as he had refound it; it could have been a one-time-only, emergency-situation type of deal. The jury was still out on that one, his dad said (probably because he was a lawyer).

Malik? He hadn't been able to see any of the ghosts he and Zack had bumped into under the school. Zack figured it was because Malik was too smart: His rational brain overrode any irrational woo-woo junk trying to creep in.

Azalea? She'd been out to lunch mentally when all the ghosts started popping up. The jury was still out on her, too.

And Zipper? Zip saw everything Zack saw, maybe more. Every once in a while, the dog would sit in the middle of a room, staring at a blank wall, and Zack knew his dog had spotted some sort of spirit lurking behind the plasterboard.

"Come on, you guys," said Judy when the car was parked. "Let's go pick some pumpkins. Ones with good shapes for scary faces!"

Zipper barked in agreement.

It was his "hurry up and let me out" bark. It'd been a long car ride, so he wanted to find a pumpkin, too.

One shaped like a fire hydrant.

13

"So, have you heard from your dad?" Judy asked Azalea as they picked their way through the patch looking for their perfect pumpkin.

"Yeah," said Azalea, whose father was in the army. "His deployment is almost up. He'll be stateside in time for Christmas."

"That's great," said Zack, who was pulling a little red wagon loaded with the two tumbling pumpkins he and Malik had already chosen because they were exactly what they were looking for: tall and oblong, perfect for carving a Frankenstein face or, in Malik's case, the silhouette of a headless horseman galloping on his thundering steed while holding his head high above his shoulders.

Malik liked to carve.

Zipper was also riding in the wagon, his front paws perched on top of one of the pumpkins so he could stand up and ride his chariot like he was a pharaoh hound.

"Mrs. Jennings?" said Malik.

"Yes?"

"Zack and I have already selected our jack-o'-lanterns."

"Oh. Do you guys want to go grab some cider or something?"

"No, thank you," said Malik. "I'm more interested in attacking that corn maze."

"Really?" said Zack. "Didn't you get enough maze running a couple weeks ago?"

"You know me," said Malik. "I love a puzzle and a fresh challenge."

True. When Zack first met Malik, he was working two Sudokus at once.

"Would you like to join us in the maze, Azalea?" Malik asked.

"Nah. I still need to find my pumpkin or one of those mangel-wurzels."

"Hang on," said Judy. "We should probably all do the maze if that's where Zack's going."

"You don't have to," said Zack, who loved his stepmom but didn't want her babysitting him all the time. "You and Azalea should go find your pumpkins."

"You sure, Zack? Your father and I are a little worried."

"About what?"

"Well, it's almost Halloween."

"So?"

"You see ghosts," Malik whispered. "Remember?"

"I know, but . . ."

"What?" said Azalea. "Do the spirits of the dead really swarm out of their graves for Halloween?"

"I think so," said Judy.

"Today's not Halloween," said Zack.

"Well," said Judy, "take Zip. Just in case you run into an early riser."

"Fine," said Zack.

Zipper hopped out of the wagon, his tail wagging.

"Azalea and I will meet you guys over there at the cider stand. And, Zack, if you see anything . . . or anybody . . ."

"All we're gonna see is a bunch of dead cornstalks. Come on, Malik."

"Remember," said Malik, "if we take nothing but right turns, we'll easily find our way to the exit."

"Okay," said Zack. They'd been wandering around inside the dusty labyrinth for about twenty minutes. "Um, maybe we should check out the map they gave you back at the start."

"I didn't take one," Malik said proudly as they trudged up a muddy tractor path. "There's really no need for a map if you already know how to solve the puzzle. Right turn!"

"Right."

Zack was wondering if maybe they should try taking a couple of left turns. He sensed they were somewhere in the middle of the maze. He glanced up at the bright blue sky, hoping the sun might give him a hint as to what direction they were heading, but it was noon, so the sun was directly overhead. Against its blazingly bright light, Zack saw a black crow circling the cornfield. He figured that was why the maze needed so many scarecrow decorations.

"You know," said Zack, "I haven't seen any other people for like five minutes."

"Because they all got lost," said Malik. "Right turn."

"Right."

Zack followed Malik around another bend and up to a T intersection.

They were facing a solid wall of withered corn.

Before Malik could say "Right turn" again, a dead man with a watermelon-sized head walked straight out of the cornstalks like those baseball players in that movie—only this wasn't Iowa and the guy wasn't there to play ball.

Zipper snarled.

The ghost grinned. His teeth were an Indian corn checkerboard of browns and blacks.

"Trick or treat, smell my feet. Give me something good to eat." He hawked up a big laugh. "Hello again, kid."

"Hello, Mad Dog," said Zack.

"Pardon?" said Malik, about to follow the path to the right.

Zack gestured at Mad Dog Murphy, a notorious (and very dead) criminal from the 1950s. Malik, of course, couldn't see the guy, or the metal helmet from the electric chair sizzling on top of his stubbly head.

"Is it a ghost?" gasped Malik.

Zack nodded.

The crow floating overhead in lazy circles started to laugh: "Haw-haw-haw."

"So," said Mad Dog, "where is it?"

"Where's what?" said Zack.

"The thingamajig."

"Huh?"

"Come on, kid. Barnabas already figured out you're a Jennings. Word to the wise? You shouldn't spend so much time in graveyards. You do, dead people pick up stuff, learn things you don't want 'em learnin'."

"I have absolutely no idea what you're talking about."

"What's he saying?" asked Malik.

"Nothing," said Zack.

"Nothing?" snarled Mad Dog, his chest swelling.

This was the first time Zack had seen Mr. Murphy when he wasn't sitting down, strapped into his electric chair, the one they'd executed him in at the state penitentiary back in 1959. The guy had to be at least seven feet tall.

"Look, kid—Little Paulie's a pal of mine. We holed up in that barn over there once when the cops was chasin' us. Good times. Now Paulie wants out. So give his people what they're looking for. Or else."

Mad Dog Murphy vanished.

In his place, Zack could see the shadow of the circling bird. When he looked up, the crow's wings stretched out wide as it swooped into dive-bomb mode—aiming straight for Zack.

"Crow!" Zack shouted.

"Actually," said Malik, "I believe that's a raven. Note the wedge shape of its tail feathers and . . ."

"Come on!" Zack grabbed Malik and they started running up the alley of corn. Zipper was hot on their heels.

"Zack?" yelled Malik. "Ravens often attack small dogs!"

Zack bent down and grabbed Zipper off the ground. "Shortcut!" he shouted.

Dog in arms, Malik right behind him, Zack mowed through the walls of the maze, trampling down crispy, crackly cornstalks, plowing forward till they finally came out in a muddy field right beside an inflatable light-up pumpkin the size of a small toolshed.

Zack glanced over his shoulder.

The big black bird pulled up, banked left, and shot off toward the horizon.

"Haw-haw-haw!" It was still laughing at them.

"Hey, Malik?" said Zack, catching his breath and brushing corn crap off his clothes.

"Yeah?"

"Let's not tell Judy about this, okay?"

"Why not?"

"Well, if we do, I think my mom and dad might lock me in my room till I turn thirteen."

"Is that when ghosts leave kids alone, when they turn thirteen?"

"I hope so," said Zack with a sigh. "I hope so."

15

Later that afternoon, Norman Ickes stood behind the counter at Ickes & Son Hardware on Main Street, fidgeting with his brand-new Nut Case, a shiny brass puzzle that looked like two hexagonal nuts screwed around the center of a half-inch bolt that had one head at the top and another at the bottom.

"It looks simple, but it isn't," he said to his young customer, a fellow puzzle maven named Malik Sherman, who was well on his way to Nerdsville, a neighborhood where Norman Ickes had lived for most of his twenty-four miserable years. "The goal is to remove the small nut hidden inside the hollow bolt without cutting the whole thing open with a hacksaw."

"Have you figured out the solution yet?" asked Malik.

"No." Now even Malik, a fellow loser, was working his nerves. He wished the kid would butt out and let him fidget in peace.

"Well, good luck with it, Norman. My dad and I are

here looking for pumpkin-carving tools. I picked out a doozy this morning down at Paproski's Pumpkin Patch."

"Will you be carving a jack-o'-lantern or something a bit more interesting, say a Halloween scene sculpted in silhouette?"

"Definitely a silhouette," said Malik. "Much more challenging and, therefore, rewarding."

Norman nodded. Any idiot could take a butcher knife and slice triangle eyes and a row of jagged teeth into a hollowed-out gourd. It took skill, patience, and the proper tools to create a pumpkin masterpiece.

"Aisle two. Seasonal items."

"Awesome. Thanks, Norman! Catch you later."

The kid bounded over to aisle two. Norman reached into the plastic pumpkin on the counter and palmed a few more pieces of candy corn. The high-fructose sugar rush helped him focus.

Concentrating intensely, Norman worked the two center nuts around and around, then dabbed at the perspiration beading up on his forehead with the tip of his green striped tie, the one his mother had given him for Christmas. It had come in a box with a matching short-sleeve green shirt. A prepackaged, easy-to-wrap combo.

"Whatcha doin', Nor-man?"

Norman looked up and saw an idiot grinning at him.

It was his coworker with the shaved head, the no-neck Neanderthal Stephen Snertz, whose young cousins,

Norman had learned, terrorized all the children of any intelligence at Malik Sherman's middle school.

Stephen Snertz had droopy eyes and half a goatee neatly trimmed on his chin. Judging by his very consistent stubble, he apparently shaved his upper lip and cheeks whenever he shaved his head.

Why Norman's dad had hired this moron to work in the Ickes & Son family hardware store, Norman would never know.

Maybe because Snertz had been the star of the high school football team six years ago, back when Norman had been president of the chess club.

Maybe because Norman's dad was a bigger wimp than Norman, always letting people push him around. His father even let Snertz keep a Smith & Wesson pistol tucked under the counter near the cash register for "security purposes."

"What kind of screwy bolt is that, you nut?" said Snertz, raiding the plastic pumpkin, scooping up every last piece of candy corn.

"It's a brainteaser."

Something you'll never need, he wanted to add, *seeing how you don't have a brain.*

"Norman?" It was his father.

"Yes, Dad?"

"Oh, hello, Stephen."

Snertz snorted snot up his nostrils. "Good afternoon, Herman."

Norman's father, Herman Ickes, was a timid man. He

was barely five feet tall, and what little hair he had left on his head had gone white when he was in his late thirties. Everything scared him. His ulcers had ulcers.

"Norman, if you don't mind, could you run down to the cellar? Mrs. Floyd is looking for an eight-foot stepladder."

"Sure, Dad."

"Thank you. Stephen?"

"Yeah, Herm?"

"Perhaps you can lend Norman a hand with the ladder?"

"Nah." He popped a fistful of candy corn into his mouth. "I'm on my break."

"Oh. I see. Sorry. I didn't realize."

"Yeah, well now you do."

"Right." Norman's dad peeled another antacid tablet off his foil-wrapped roll. "Well, I'll be in my office."

"Great," said Snertz. "I'll be in the back. With the appliances."

Norman rolled his eyes. That meant Snertz would be watching college football on TV for the rest of the afternoon while Norman hauled stepladders up from the cellar.

Ten minutes later, Norman was ringing up Mrs. Jessie Floyd at the cash register.

Stephen Snertz was in the back of the store, screaming at the TV screens.

Apparently, one of the referees was an idiot.

Norman's dad was still in his office. With the door locked. He liked to hide in there a lot.

"Can you help me carry this to my car?" asked Mrs. Floyd, who was about sixty years old.

"I guess," said Norman. He came out from behind the counter and hoisted the eight-foot stepladder off the floor. The thing felt like it weighed five hundred pounds, even though the sticker on its side claimed it only weighed twenty-six point two. "Stephen? Watch the register. I'm helping Mrs. Floyd."

"What?" Snertz shouted, unable to hear him over the roar of eight different football games on eight different TVs.

So Norman swung around to repeat himself.

The ladder swung with him and took out the display racks in front of the counter. Rolls of duct tape went flying.

Norman spun back around.

This time, he took out everything stacked on top of the counter: washers, wing nuts, the disco-dancing Frankenstein doll, the plastic pumpkin, and the entire key and key ring rack.

"Smooth move, Ex-Lax!" shouted Snertz. "What a wimp. Just like your old man!"

Head down, Norman Ickes shuffled out the front door, toting Mrs. Floyd's ladder.

She was snickering at him, too.

Norman's shoulders sagged.

Stephen Snertz was right.

He was a wimp. Just like his father.

They should call their hardware store Wimp & Son. Better yet, Wimp & Wimpier.

16

People were gawking at Jenny Ballard as she drifted up the sidewalks of Main Street.

They weren't used to seeing anyone walking around North Chester in a hooded cape. She passed two young boys, maybe ten or twelve years old, sipping soft drinks and straddling their bikes.

"Hey, witch lady," said the chubby one. "Aren't you a little early? Halloween isn't until Monday!"

Jenny turned to glare at the boys. Smiling devilishly, she wondered what the chubby one might look like as a honey-baked ham or, perhaps, a donkey.

Unfortunately, she hadn't learned those spells yet.

Besides, she had work to do. For the voice!

She continued up Main Street, past the town clock tower, past the Hedge Pig Emporium (a shop that sold herbs and extracts to crunchy granola–type people), past the North Chester Book Nook and Yankee Doodle Dry Cleaners.

All the stores had posters in their windows for something called Nightmare on Main Street—a Halloween Fun Fest. Sounded pretty lame to Jenny.

When she reached the Ickes & Son Hardware store, she suddenly stopped.

"Bring him to us on All Hallows' Eve!" whispered the strange crow's voice in her head.

She glanced through the plate-glass window.

Saw a nerdy guy in an ugly tie cleaning up a mess on the floor.

"Bring him to us!"

"Him?" Jenny said out loud.

"Him!"

"They land first thing tomorrow morning," said Zack's father. "Bradley Airport."

"It'll be good to see them again," said Judy. "Um, could you remind me of their names? I met so many people at the wedding."

"Sure. Aunt Hannah—she's the oldest—Aunt Sophie, and Aunt Ginny. Ginny's the youngest."

"How young?" asked Zack, who vaguely remembered meeting three little old ladies at his real mom's funeral and then at his dad and Judy's wedding.

"Aunt Ginny is seventy-seven."

Oh, yeah, thought Zack. *She's practically an infant.*

Zack, Judy, and his dad were sitting in the dining room, passing around a pizza box. This was their usual Saturday dinner. It was easy for Judy to fix; all she had to do was pick up the phone. Zipper was hunkered down beneath the table, ready to pounce on any stray pepperonis that fell his way.

"I guess you should probably call them Aunt Hannah, Aunt Sophie, and Aunt Ginny, too, Zack," his dad said, "even though, technically, they're your *great*-aunts. And, Zack?"

"Yeah?"

"They're nothing like Aunt Francine."

Aunt Francine was his real mother's sister. She had always hated Zack.

"These three are your good aunts."

Zack smiled. "I thought you said they were my *great* aunts."

His dad laughed. "They are. Especially Ginny. You'll see. They'll stay with us for a few days and then head back to Florida."

"Um, Dad?"

"Yeah, Zack?"

"Why exactly are they coming?"

"Remember how I told you I used to see ghosts when I was your age?"

"Yeah."

"Well, Aunt Ginny was the only one I could talk to about it."

"How come?"

"My mother had already passed away and my dad was too busy, being sheriff and all. Besides, I figured he'd just think I was a big baby if I told him the truth."

Zack could relate. He'd felt the same way. It was why he only told his dad about his "gift" after his father had already seen it in action.

"Anyway, after I talked to Aunt Ginny—poof! The ghosts left me alone."

"I thought that happened when you turned thirteen," said Judy.

"Right. Aunt Ginny and I talked on my birthday; dead people never bothered me again."

"Zack?" said Judy.

"Yeah?"

"We know you don't need Aunt Ginny or anybody to babysit you. But with Halloween coming, your dad and I figured we should take some extra precautions. Besides, Aunt Ginny's family. She'll have your best interests at heart."

Zack raised an eyebrow.

Judy knew about Zack's real mother. How she had belittled and berated him. Susan Potter Jennings had never, ever had Zack's best interests at heart.

"I think Aunt Ginny will be different, hon," said Judy.

Zack nodded. "Okay."

"Great," said his dad.

"We're going to need the two guest bedrooms plus your room while they're here," said Judy. "You and Zipper okay with camping out down in the rumpus room?"

"Sure," said Zack.

The rumpus room was where he had his video games hooked up to their old TV. There was also a mini-fridge stocked with soft drinks and chocolate milk, plus a microwave oven for popcorn.

"I guess Zip and I can rough it on the couch down there for a couple nights."

"Great," said Judy.

"Their plane lands at nine," said his dad. "You want to ride out to the airport with me, Zack?"

"Sure."

His father chuckled. "They'll probably have a ton of luggage. They always do. They might even bring their cats."

"Cats?" said Judy.

"Yeah. They each have one."

Under the table, Zipper grumbled.

He sounded like he was looking forward to this visit about as much as Zack was.

18

On Sunday morning, Zack and his dad stood in the baggage claim area at Connecticut's Bradley Airport, waiting for the aunts to arrive.

All sorts of people were milling around, staring up at the arrivals monitor or over at the hallway where the passengers on flight 33 from Miami would soon appear.

Zack saw a strangely dressed young airplane pilot wandering around the empty baggage carousel. Judging by his uniform, Zack knew he didn't work for any of the airlines.

The guy was wearing a World War II flight suit and a goggled helmet. He also had a cockpit seat strapped to his butt. Whenever he walked past someone in the crowd, they would shiver like they just drank a Slurpee too fast.

Nobody but Zack saw the ghost of the World War II flying ace.

Well, the dog working with the security patrol probably saw him, but it was too busy sniffing stuff to snarl at the antique aviator.

Zack's dad, who the guy almost bumped into as he loped around the baggage carousel, didn't see the pilot, proving that he had once again lost his ghost-seeing abilities.

"Georgie?" yodeled a sweet voice. "Yoo-hoo. Georgie?"

The ghost vanished.

Zack turned around and saw three white-haired ladies toddling up the wide terminal in a flying wedge formation. The yodeling one, the one in the middle, was wearing a flowery dress and hiking boots. Smiling and laughing, she stretched her arms out wide.

"Oh, Georgie! Let me look at you. You're a sight for sore eyes!"

"You too, Aunt Ginny!" They hugged. Zack smelled petunias. Aunt Ginny must like flowery perfume.

"Hello, Zachary," said the tall aunt on the left. She looked as brittle as stick candy and had more wrinkles on her face than Zack had in his pajamas.

"Oh me, oh my," giggled the chubby one on the right, who had bazoombas the size of Paproski's prizewinning pumpkins. "Hello, Zachary, hello!" She squeezed his cheeks. "You're so cute, I could gobble you up."

Zack smiled even though she looked like she might actually eat children for breakfast. With syrup and lots of butter.

"You've certainly grown since the wedding," said the tall one very matter-of-factly.

"He sure has, Aunt Hannah," said Zack's dad.

"Must be eating right," said the pudgy one with the pillow chest.

"Zack, you remember Aunt Ginny, Aunt Sophie, and Aunt Hannah?"

"Uh, yeah. Hi."

"And how's Judy?" gushed Aunt Ginny.

"Great. She's at home."

"Is she fixing breakfast?" asked Aunt Sophie, eagerly fluttering her eyelids behind her gigantically round glasses. "They only fed us sugar cookies and peanuts on the plane. Will there be snacks in the car, Georgie?"

"First things first," said Aunt Hannah, who Zack figured was the boss. "Where is our luggage?" She glared at the unmoving baggage conveyor belt. "We had to pay to check our bags. Having paid, you'd think—"

An air horn blared three times and an alarm bell rang.

The conveyor belt started up. Suitcases immediately slid down the chute.

"Oh, goody!" said Sophie. "Here come our trunks."

"Come on, Zack," said his dad. "Give me a hand here."

Zack and his dad stepped up to the conveyor belt. Three antique footlockers, the kind magicians and cruise passengers pack their gear in, trundled down the chute.

"Those are ours," decreed Hannah.

"And those, too," said Aunt Ginny, gesturing toward three hefty satchels made out of paisley-swirled carpet and clasped at the top with fancy brass hardware.

"You sure you ladies packed enough?" Zack's dad asked as he heaved the first trunk off the carousel.

"Well," said Ginny, "we didn't know exactly what we might need, so we packed everything."

"What Virginia meant to say," said Aunt Hannah, "is that your weather up here is rather unpredictable, much different from what we enjoy down in Florida."

"Oh, yes," Aunt Sophie chimed in. "That's what Virginia meant to say. It's the weather. We brought several different wardrobes."

"By wardrobes, do you mean furniture?" Zack's dad joked. "These things are heavier than a chest of drawers!"

Zack helped his dad lug the second trunk onto a rolling cart.

"And here comes our most precious cargo!" chirped Aunt Ginny as an airline porter rolled a wagon carrying three pet carriers toward them. "Our kitties!"

"So you brought all your cats?" said Zack's dad.

"Heavens, no," sniffed Hannah. "Just the three who aren't afraid to fly."

Once the trunks and bags and cats were loaded into the back of the family van, Zack and his dad helped the elderly aunts step up into the vehicle.

Aunt Hannah, claiming seniority, would be riding shotgun.

Zack sat in the back on the bench seat, sandwiched between ginormous Aunt Sophie and smiling Aunt Ginny. Actually, Sophie was so wide-bottomed, Zack and Ginny were basically sharing the right half of the bench.

"'Bradley Airport,'" said Aunt Ginny, reading the big road sign as they drove past it. "'Welcome to Connecticut. The Constitution State. Enjoy Your Visit.' Do you read billboards, Zack?"

"Well, not out loud . . ."

"Oh, it's an excellent way to sharpen one's reading skills, don't you think?"

"I guess."

"Do you know why they call this Bradley Airport?"

Aunt Ginny was beaming at Zack the way a good teacher does, the kind who wants you to learn everything she already knows.

"No, ma'am."

"Well, that's all right. Very few people in Connecticut do. You see, the airfield was named after a World War II fighter pilot named Eugene Bradley, a young man from Antlers, Oklahoma, who, during a training exercise, crashed his plane in the woods just north of here."

"Really?"

"Oh, yes. Lieutenant Bradley was the first fatality at what, in 1941, was a brand-new army air base."

"Neat. So, how come you know all this stuff?"

"Don't forget, dear: Hannah, Sophie, and I grew up in North Chester with your grandpa Jim."

"Right."

Now Aunt Ginny leaned in closer and covered her mouth so she and Zack could share a secret.

"I also think the plane crash is why Lieutenant Bradley is forever pacing around that baggage carousel. He must be looking for his lost flight bag."

Zack's eyes widened.

Aunt Ginny winked.

She'd seen the pilot with the seat strapped to his seat, too!

20

"Oh, my!" gushed Aunt Sophie. "This food tastes delicious! Mmm!"

The whole family, all six Jenningses, was seated around the big dining room table, which Judy had decorated with gourds, a couple of carved pumpkins, and dried leaves to give it a real Halloween feel.

She of course hadn't spent nearly as much time cooking as she had decorating, because she was less likely to set off the smoke detector decorating. Judy had picked up dinner at the closest chain restaurant where they brought your food to the parking lot.

"I have now read all of your Curiosity Cat books, Judy," said Aunt Ginny. "They're quite good. I would imagine it's not easy telling an amusing, entertaining, and educational tale with so few words."

"That's right," said Zack's dad. "That's why Judy's won so many awards."

"Well, this garlic herb chicken deserves an award, too," said Ginny. "It's scrumptious. Absolutely scrumptious."

"Mmm-hmmm," added Aunt Sophie, her mouth full of mashed potatoes. "Scrumdillyicious."

"Thank you," said Judy. "It's our neighbor Mrs. Applebee's secret recipe."

"And where does this Applebee family live?" asked Hannah, who, Zack had quickly discovered, didn't have much of a sense of humor. (Hannah hadn't liked it much when Aunt Ginny and Zack swapped gross-out jokes on the ride home from the airport.)

"So," said Zack's dad, trying to change the subject, "are your rooms okay, ladies?"

"Fine," said Sophie, tearing open a roll.

"They'll do," said Hannah.

"The pillows could be fluffier, I suppose," said Sophie, slathering a gob of butter on her roll.

"And, of course, I'm allergic to feathers," added Hannah.

"Well, my room is marvelous!" said Ginny.

"You got my bedroom," said Zack.

"Really? Where are you sleeping?"

"Downstairs. With Zipper."

Zipper was out in the backyard, probably hunkered down inside his doghouse, strategizing the best way to do battle with the newly arrived cats, all of which came equipped with the "claws of fury" feature.

"We may need to do some shopping," pronounced Aunt Hannah. "After all, tomorrow is Halloween."

"We already have candy to hand out," said Judy. "Miniature Butterfingers and Baby Ruths."

"And where do you store those?" asked Aunt Sophie, fluttering her eyelids again.

"Sophia?" scolded Hannah.

"Sorry."

"We need to purchase certain items at the Hedge Pig Emporium to aid Zachary with his paranormal proclivities."

Zack figured "paranormal proclivities" meant he could see ghosts.

"I trust the Hedge Pig is still open, George?"

"Yes, Aunt Hannah," said Zack's dad. "I think so. I haven't thought about that old place in ages."

"Good. That is how it should be."

"Oh, yes," echoed Sophie. "Indeed. As it should be."

"We went to the Hedge Pig Emporium on your birthday once. Remember, Georgie?" said Aunt Ginny.

"Really?"

"The ladies in the back made you a milk shake. Chocolate, if I recall."

"Oh, right. When I turned thirteen."

Aunt Ginny winked at Zack again.

His dad's thirteenth birthday was when he had stopped seeing ghosts. Zack wondered if it was just a coincidence or if the Hedge Pig people used Ghostbusters ice cream in their milk shakes.

21

Malik and Azalea came over to Zack's house around six.

It was already dark out.

They joined Zack and Aunt Ginny downstairs in the rumpus room, where Zack was teaching the seventy-seven-year-old how to play Madden NFL Football on his PlayStation 3. Judy and Zack's dad were at the mall with Aunts Hannah and Sophie, hoping to find "more suitable pillows."

And a hot water bottle.

Aunt Sophie wanted one of those, even though Zack had no idea why anybody would want to drink their water hot.

Zipper was down in the basement, too—basically lying low. When a cat slapped you five, it hurt. Especially if they slapped you a face five.

"I need help putting together my Halloween costume," said Azalea, slumping down into a beat-up old recliner, while, on the couch, Aunt Ginny thumbed her controller and power-smacked Zack's quarterback into fumbling the ball.

"I'm all set," said Malik, who was sitting on the floor, Zipper's head in his lap. "I'm going as a killer bee."

"Huh?" said Zack, watching Aunt Ginny's lineman on the TV screen as he scooped up the fumbled football and scored a touchdown.

"I cut a big letter 'B' out of yellow poster board and splattered it with red paint. I will, of course, also carry a bloody rubber knife."

"Clever," said Azalea. "A killer 'B.' Wish I'd thought of that."

Aunt Ginny put down her game controller. "So, Azalea. What would *you* like to . . . *be?*"

Azalea chuckled. "I dunno. I was thinking about maybe a gypsy or the bride of Dracula."

"Both very good choices, dear. I have an idea: Why don't you three run upstairs and rummage through my trunk? I brought along all sorts of scarves and skirts, bangles and baubles."

"May I ask why?" inquired Malik.

"Well, dear, I never unpack my footlocker. Just keep stuffing new items into it as I continue my journey through life's grand adventure. Why, I haven't emptied that trunk since the 1970s! It's filled with things I have long since forgotten."

"So why do you keep them, then?" asked Azalea.

"Because, dear, you just never know when a new friend might need a quick Halloween costume."

22

It *looked* like an underwear bomb had gone off in Zack's bedroom.

A gigantic bra was draped over his desk chair. A pair of flowery underpants, the size of a bathroom rug, lay on the floor. Some other lacy stuff, embroidered with flowers and butterflies, spilled out of his dresser drawers.

Azalea found a crystal spray bottle on top of Zack's bedside table and spritzed it.

Then she started coughing and choking.

"Old-person perfume alert," she gasped. "Total gag juice."

"Look at all this neat junk!" said Malik, who was merrily rummaging through the summer-camp-sized footlocker, the sides of which were stickered with decals from exotic locations. "Scarves, hats, costume jewelry, a turban of some sort, leather-bound books, a pouch full of sparkling powder, a whole box of white candles or flares or something . . ."

Zack and Azalea knelt down on the carpet beside Malik and started going through the stuff with him. Zipper hadn't joined them on the trek upstairs. He was on cat-attack alert down in the rumpus room with Aunt Ginny, who had announced that she might take a quick "snoozle on the couch," which, she explained, was the same thing as a nap.

Pyewacket, Aunt Ginny's cat, who had been sleeping in a lump under the bed's comforter, came padding over to the trunk and hopped inside the box to help the three friends paw through the layers of fascinating junk.

"Don't tell Zipper," said Azalea, "but I think cats are awesome."

"Me too," said Malik, stroking the pink-nosed cat on her head.

"This is so cool," said Azalea, pulling out a turban and trying it on. "I could be like a gypsy mind reader."

"Yeah," said Zack. "Look—here's a deck of tarot cards to go with it."

"And this star necklace would work, too," said Malik. "It's a pentagram, because it has five points, the same way a pentagon has five sides."

Azalea draped the pendant around her neck. "So, Zack?"

"Yeah?"

"What are you going to go as for Halloween?"

"Oh. I'm not sure. I mean, I don't know."

"Huh?"

"I may not get to go trick-or-treating this year."

"What?"

"You know—the ghost thing. Halloween being their busiest night and all. That's why my aunts are here."

"To go trick-or-treating for you?" said Malik.

"No. My dad said Aunt Ginny helped him a bunch, back when he was a kid and could see ghosts. Thinks maybe she can help me."

"Hey, you guys," said Azalea. "I have an idea—what if we just do that Nightmare on Main Street deal? I don't think any ghosts could hurt you there, not with that many people around."

"Yeah," said Zack. "My dad suggested that, too. You guys wouldn't think it's too lame?"

"Uh, no," said Azalea. "Not if there's free candy. Stores always give out the best junk, anyway. Oh, this is so cool!" She pulled a large crystal shaped like a cat out of the trunk. "This could be my gypsy mind reader's familiar."

"What's a familiar?" asked Malik.

"It's an animal that helps a witch or a magician."

"Fascinating," said Malik. "I did not know that."

"I read a lot of Wiccan crap like that during my Goth phase."

Pyewacket meowed at Malik.

"Wow!" he said.

"What?" said Zack and Azalea.

"Check out this nifty puzzle!" Malik held up what looked like a polished black stone heart. "It was buried near the bottom. The cat found it."

"What exactly is it?" asked Azalea. "I mean, besides black?"

78

"An interlocking puzzle. You can see the seams between pieces. Also, if you look at the center, you'll see the smoky outer shell is somewhat translucent and there is another tiny black heart in the middle of the big black heart."

"So the object is to remove the small heart?" asked Azalea.

"Precisely."

Malik rubbed his fingers together and then clasped the rounded top on the right side of the heart. Pyewacket, who was perched on the lid of the trunk, purred.

"There!" he said as the first piece slid out. "That has released this next piece." Out came the V-shaped bottom. "Which unlocks this piece."

A dozen twists and turns later, Malik had taken the black stone heart completely apart and freed the tiny coal-black heart trapped at its core.

"Well done, puzzle geek," said Azalea playfully.

"Why, thank you," said Malik. "Hey, Zack, do you think your aunt Ginny would mind if I shared this with a friend, a fellow puzzle aficionado?"

"You mean a fellow geek," said Azalea.

Zack shrugged. "Sure. Why not? I mean, she has so much junk in this trunk, I don't think she'll miss one puzzle."

The three friends continued laughing and digging through Aunt Ginny's treasure chest.

Which was why none of them heard the low rumble of thunder from somewhere not too far up the road.

23

The dog that men called the Black Shuck had been sent to guard the Haddam Hill Cemetery, to protect the goodly souls buried there from the graveyard's foulest residents.

It perked up its ears, not liking what it heard.

The click of a lock being opened.

A spell being broken.

The dog scurried around to the front of the Ickleby crypt.

The black heart lock was still there, clamped tight through the hasp on the door.

But the dog smelled something foul.

The pent-up evil of thirteen villainous souls seeping out through the crypt's mildewed stone walls.

The seal had been shattered.

The souls of the Icklebys had, somehow, been set free.

Zack was having another very bad dream.

He figured it was because he was sleeping in the basement on a flimsy foldout sofa bed with a metal bar digging into his spine.

Or maybe because of the ice cream sundaes he and Aunt Ginny had whipped up in the kitchen after Malik and Azalea had gone home: Moose Tracks and peppermint ice cream topped with fudge sauce, raw cookie dough (squeezed straight from the tube), a gob of peanut butter, whipped cream, and maraschino cherries. Plus sprinkles.

Yeah. That'd give a guy nightmares.

In the dream, things kept turning into other things. First Zack and Zipper were floating downstream in a big and bouncy bra boat. They each had their own foamy bucket seat lined with frilly lace. But then the bra boat became a double-barrel slingshot, which Zack's pal Davy, who popped in to say, "Howdy, pardner," used to make trick shots behind his back, one of which took out a window on Main Street, which was when Grandpa Jim, in his sheriff's uniform, showed up.

"Zack?" said Grandpa Jim. "Are you awake, champ?"

Zack pried open an eye.

Grandpa Jim was sitting in the battered recliner where Azalea had sat earlier, a chair Zack's dad had inherited when Grandpa Jim passed away.

"Don't worry, champ. I'll be keeping an eye on things."

"What kind of things?"

"Anything. Everything."

"What exactly are you talking about, Grandpa?"

"Can't say."

"Because of the rules?"

Grandpa Jim nodded.

From the other ghosts he'd met, Zack had learned that there were very strict rules governing what ghosts could do or say to help people on the other side of the dirt, and since Grandpa Jim had been the top cop in North Chester when he was alive, he was all about playing by the rules.

"Are you here to protect me from evil spirits?"

Grandpa Jim gave Zack a worried smile that told Zack that, yep, that was exactly why he had popped in so close to Halloween.

"That's why your sisters are here, too," said Zack. "All of them. Ginny, Sophie, and Hannah."

"I know."

"They're upstairs if you want to say hello."

"Already did."

"Are you here to protect them, too?"

"Those three don't need me, Zack. Go back to sleep, champ. There's nothing for you to do. Not tonight, anyway."

"Tomorrow's Halloween. Is that when the trouble starts?"

"Can't say."

"Because they won't let you?"

"Because I don't know what tomorrow might bring. Nobody does."

"Okay. So what am I supposed to do?"

"Same thing I told you to do that time I took you fishing up at Coulter's Pond."

Coulter's Pond was a lake where everybody said Battling Bob, this bigmouthed bass the size of a whale, lurked just below the surface, waiting to yank unsuspecting fishermen out of their boats.

"Um, you told me to sit down because I was rocking the boat?"

"And after that?"

"You said I should hold on to my fishing rod real tight, just in case Battling Bob was itching for a fight."

"That's right, Zack. Be ready and hang on tight."

And with that, Grandpa Jim Jennings disappeared into the cushions of his favorite chair.

25

A half mile up the road, thirteen devilish souls swarmed together outside the buttressed stone walls of the Ickleby family crypt, savoring their newfound freedom.

"The foul curse is finally broken!" proclaimed Barnabas.

"Hang on, Pops," said Eddie Boy Ickleby, the murdering thief who had died in 1979. His shaggy hair was cut into a mullet—short in the front and on the sides, long in the back. "The black heart lock is still clamped tight to the door, man."

"It was never the lock that held us prisoner," said Barnabas. "It was something much stronger." His mask—a jack-o'-lantern pattern cut into a coarse burlap sack—was cinched around his neck with a frayed rope as thick as any hangman's noose.

"What're you bumping your gums about?" demanded the 1930s gangster ghost, Crazy Izzy Ickleby.

"The sinister spell of the three detestable Jennings

sisters," said Barnabas. "They were the ones who sealed our souls inside this wretched tomb with their cursed incantations."

The spirits now circled around Barnabas were his direct descendants: Silas Ickleby, in his powdered wig; Webley Ickleby, the most notorious mass murderer of the 1820s; Pie-Eyes Ickleby, who had rushed to California in 1849, not to mine for gold but to steal it from those who did; Little Paulie Ickleby, who, with Mad Dog Murphy, had robbed banks during the 1950s.

"Do you suppose those three sisters might lock us up once again?" This came from Hornus Ickleby, a scallywag who, like so many of these thirteen Icklebys, had met his death at the noosed end of a rope.

"Rest easy, gentlemen," hissed Barnabas. "We simply need to seize the black heart stone before the Jennings sisters reassemble it and repeat their abominable spell!"

"Seize it?" snarled Cornelius Ickleby, an embezzler who, in the late 1800s, had devised clever Wall Street swindles. He was crouched near a fallen branch. "Look here—I cannot even seize this twig lying before me on the ground. My hands pass clean through it."

"You idle-headed, inky-fingered clerk," sneered Barnabas. "As ghosts, we can do little. To thrive, we must find a living, breathing body!"

"Say what, Old Scratch?" said Bad Bart Ickleby, a riverboat gambler who had died with five aces up his sleeve.

"He's right, man," said Eddie Boy. "We gotta find us a new body."

"How we gonna do that, huh, huh?" demanded Crazy Izzy.

Barnabas smirked beneath his mask. "Do not worry, children. A fresh body will come to us when the veil between our world and theirs is at its thinnest."

"And when exactly is that?"

"Today!" croaked Barnabas. "Halloween."

26

Halloween fell on a Monday, so at two-thirty in the afternoon, Zack was still at school.

"The same middle school where his father used to chat with the dead crossing guard," said Ginny. "The same school where Zack recently ran into the ghost of Horace P. Pettimore."

"We must put an end to all this," said Hannah. "Immediately."

"Oh, yes," echoed Sophie. "We surely must. Right after supper."

Zack's three great-aunts stood huddled around the cold barbecue grill on the deck. Zack's dad was working at his office in New York City. Judy had gone to the mall to pick up some last-minute costume accessories for Zack and his friends.

Only Zipper remained at home with the three sisters, and he was hunkered down inside his doghouse, keeping one eye on the three elderly women, the other on the three cats circling their ankles.

27

Zipper didn't like this.

It was bad. Very, very, very bad.

Three cats in the yard.

His yard.

A dog's backyard was his castle.

But now three cats were out on the deck, purring and stretching and sticking their fannies up in the air like they owned the place. Soon they'd be prancing down the steps to poop in the shrubs and pee under the trees. They would make Zipper's castle smell cat nasty.

This was a cat-tastrophe.

One of the cats, Mister Cookiepants, a tabby who was sort of tubby, had already stolen several pieces of kibble from Zipper's food bowl.

Another, Pyewacket, swung around and swatted him on the snout when she didn't like the way Zipper sniffed her heinie.

The third one, Mystic, the black cat, had hissed at

Zipper when he tried to steal her floppy fish toy. Mystic was bad luck and bad news.

Zipper usually liked cats. But usually, they lived somewhere else and peed and pooped in a box or some other dog's backyard.

He wondered if Pyewacket, Mister Cookiepants, and Mystic were moving in.

Would there be crystal dinner bowls filled with globs of fishy gunk?

Would he start coughing up hair balls?

Would they make him join in the chorus when they started howling at the moon?

Zipper sighed and sulked and sank his head between his paws.

He needed a plan.

Well, first he needed a nap.

He yawned and stretched and drifted off into the most wonderful dream.

It was marvelous. Better than a bacon cheeseburger wrapped in ham and served on a meat loaf bun.

Zipper was chasing hundreds of cats up trees and telephone poles.

And not a single one of them ever came back down!

28

Ginny could tell: Her big sister Hannah was, once again, ready to tell her and Sophie what they needed to do.

"There is only one sure way to protect Zachary," Hannah decreed. "We must take him to the Hedge Pig Emporium. He must drink the milk shake."

"Oh, Hannah," said Ginny. "Honestly. That's a bit dramatic, don't you think? What if Zack does not wish to give up his gift?"

"He is a boy, Virginia. He does not know what is best for him."

"And we do?" asked Ginny, arching an eyebrow.

"Of course we do. We're adults."

"Wisdom and age, dear sister, are not automatically linked."

The three cats meowed. They always did that when they heard something they agreed with.

"Could we go with Zack and order milk shakes, too?" asked Sophie, who was working open the crinkly wrapper on one of the fun-sized candy bars she had snagged from the bags Judy kept stored in the pantry.

Hannah glared at her.

"I was just curious," Sophie mumbled. "Actually, I prefer ice cream sodas. And Milky Ways." She popped one into her mouth.

"Might I remind you, sisters," said Ginny, "that the milk shake will only prove effective should Zack truly desire to free himself from these uninvited visitors?"

"It worked on his father," countered Hannah.

"Indeed it did," said Ginny. "But only after he was ready to let his gift go."

"Sisters," said Sophie, licking her chocolate-smudged fingertips, "today is Halloween. Dead souls will be popping up all over the place, searching for anybody who has the gift, anyone who can do their bidding. Oh, my—they'll be looking for Zack! They'll be looking for us!"

"We should immediately counsel Zack to make the choice," said Hannah. "To willingly drink the drink. We should do it before sundown!"

"But, dear sister," said Ginny, "what if, by taking away his gift just when he needs it most, we render Zack even more vulnerable to the demons who seek to do him harm?"

"Who?" asked Sophie, her eyes nearly bugging out of her head. "Who wants to hurt Zack?"

"Many," said Ginny. "Never forget, we three made quite a few immortal enemies when we were young and in our prime."

"Very well," sighed Hannah wearily. "What would you suggest, Virginia?"

"Yes," said Sophie, unwrapping a second candy bar. "Tell us."

"It's very simple," Ginny answered calmly. "Georgie will be taking Zack and his friends trick-or-treating on Main Street tonight. He will be surrounded by a crowd of living souls to shield him from the wandering dead."

"Being in a happy crowd often saddens deceased souls," said Hannah, "especially those who did not seize the day and enjoy life while they were living it."

"Exactly. Now then, I will go along on the excursion to offer protection in the unlikely event it should prove necessary. Afterward, Zack and I will discuss his desires. If he truly wishes to be free of his gift, then, sisters, rest assured—I shall take him to the Hedge Pig Emporium at the first opportunity and order him their thickest, richest milk shake."

Hannah nodded solemnly. "So let it be."

Ginny reached out and clasped Hannah's hand on her left, Sophie's on her right. Sophie completed the circle by joining hands with Hannah. The three cats stretched into a tails-up, heads-down bow.

"We three agree?" said Hannah.

"We three agree," chanted Sophie and Virginia in reply.

And the matter was closed to further discussion.

Around four-thirty on Halloween, Malik's and Azalea's parents dropped them off at Zack's house.

They both had a little trouble climbing out of the cars because they were already in costume: giant bright-yellow poster-board "Bs" splattered with ketchup and salsa (for chunkier blood). Zack, brandishing a bloodied rubber machete, met them on the front porch in his own big yellow "B."

"Buenos nachos, senor and senorita," said Zack in a cheesy Spanish accent, because he and Malik had read up on killer bees and learned that a bunch of them swarm north from Central and South America every year, which was also why they'd added sombreros to their costumes. Azalea had kept the gypsy turban from Aunt Ginny's trunk. She was going as the queen killer bee.

The night before, when his two friends had learned that Zack still didn't have a costume, Azalea suggested they all borrow Malik's "awesome idea" and become a hive of killer bees. Judy went to the party store at the mall and picked up three pairs of deely-boppers—those springy glitter balls on a headband—so they'd all look like they had goofy antennae bobbing around on their heads. She actually found a fourth pair at the pet store. It was for Zipper.

Zack's dad came out to the porch to join Zack, Azalea, and Malik. Aunt Ginny, dressed in a fleecy purple tracksuit and toting a small purple backpack, followed him.

"Wow, you guys look fantastic," said Zack's dad, who had caught the early train home from New York City so he could take Zack and his friends trick-or-treating. "What great costumes."

"It was Malik's idea," said Zack.

"Well, Malik, I give your killer bees an 'A.'"

Zack and Azalea groaned. Malik, on the other hand, beamed with pride.

"Thank you, Mr. Jennings," he said.

"I think you all look absolutely adorable!" gushed Aunt Ginny.

Zack, Azalea, and Malik arched their eyebrows.

"Adorable?" said Zack. "Aunt Ginny, we're splattered with blood. We're carrying bloody weapons."

"I even have blood on both my antennae," added Azalea.

"Oh, you know what, Azalea?" The seventy-seven-year-old clapped her hands together like a giddy first grader. "You should splash some blood on your turban, too. It'd look cute!"

"Um," said Zack, "*cute* isn't exactly what we were going for here, Aunt Ginny."

"After all," said Azalea, "this is Halloween. It's supposed to be the scariest night of the year."

"Oh, of course, dear," said Aunt Ginny. "My bad, as they say. Kindly allow me to rephrase my remarks: You three look absolutely horrible! In fact, you look hideous. Better?"

"Much," said Azalea with a laugh.

Judy came out to the porch with the digital camera and a bowl of miniature candy bars. Zipper was right behind her. The three "Bs" knelt down around Zip and posed for a few quick pictures. They also helped Judy hand out candy to the first pack of little kids (two Disney princesses, one Batman, and an alien) to troop up the steps while their parents stood smiling proudly down on the lawn.

"Guess we better hit Main Street," said Zack's dad. "The festivities are just about to start."

"The event officially starts at five," said Azalea. "There's a costume contest at six-thirty, doughnuts and cider at seven. I memorized the poster."

Of course she had.

"You guys all set?" asked Zack's dad.

"Sí, Senor Jennings," said Malik, only he pronounced it "Hennings," the same way "Jose" is pronounced "Hose-ay."

They trundled down the porch steps and headed for the van. Zack's dad and Aunt Ginny rode up front. Malik, Azalea, and Zack worked their way into the rear, careful not to crush or bend their stiff costumes. Zipper hopped in after them.

"Seat belts buckled?" asked Zack's dad.

"Yes," said Malik. "My motto is 'Bee prepared!' Hey, do you know what my favorite bee-movie is? *The Sting*!"

When Malik said that, even sweet Aunt Ginny groaned.

30

Main Street was packed.

Zack saw vampires and zombies; a headless football player carrying a chainsaw; a cheerleader with an axe in her back; skeletons and ninjas; pirates, witches, and Tinker Bells; and one kid who had stuck two round pumpkins in the seat of his droopy jeans so he looked like he was mooning the world with a bright-orange plumber's butt.

"This is awesome," said Malik as they pulled into a parking spot in front of a funky little health food store called the Hedge Pig Emporium. Zack and Judy had gone in there once. They sold junk like wheatgrass drinks, vitamin pills, and sugarless, wheat-free, eco-friendly, vegan carob chip brownies that tasted like baked dirt.

"Did I mention there's a one-hundred-dollar prize for best costume?" said Azalea. "So when we win it, we split it, deal?"

"Deal," said Zack.

"Where's the contest being held?" asked Malik.

"At the base of the clock tower," said Azalea, gesturing up Main Street to the intersection where the town clock, a massive stone tower, stood. The wealthy Spratling family had erected the six-story fieldstone monument because they'd run a clock company. The clock up top, however, was busted. Its scrolled iron hands stood frozen at 9:52.

"I suggest we hit the candy shop first," said Malik.

"I like the way you think," said Azalea. "Hit 'em early before they're totally cleaned out."

"Exactly."

"Um, do you guys need to come with us?" Zack asked his dad and Aunt Ginny, who were still sitting in the van.

"Oh, I don't think so," said Aunt Ginny. "None of these ghouls look all that . . . authentic."

"Yeah," said Zack.

"Why don't you guys work your way up the block?" suggested his dad. "We'll—you know—hang back."

"Cool."

"But if you see something . . ."

"I'll say something."

His dad gave him a loving smile. "Works for me."

"Come on, you guys." Zack led the charge up the sidewalk.

The owners of Main Street Sweets & Treats were giving everybody who walked through their door in costume a white bag filled with a half pound of their Halloween specialties: orange-and-yellow candy corn, those little orange pumpkins with the stubby green stems that taste just like candy corn, and Indian corn candy corn, which tasted like regular candy corn mixed with waxy chocolate. One girl who came into the store was dressed like a piece of candy corn. She got two little white bags.

After Main Street Sweets & Treats, the killer "Bs" and bumblebee Zipper (who was allowed into all the stores except the ones that sold meat) headed up the sidewalk toward Ickes & Son Hardware.

"Last year, the Ickeses gave out Almond Joys and Snickers, I heard," said Malik. "We might want to skip the dentist's office, however."

"How come?" asked Zack.

"Last year, he gave out floss."

"Was it at least spearmint-flavored floss?" asked Azalea.

Malik shook his head. "Plain. Unwaxed."

"Lame," said Azalea.

"Totally," said Zack.

A Frankenstein and a Star Wars Stormtrooper brushed past them, followed by three kids in bedsheets.

"Killer bees!" shouted one of the bedsheets. "Awesome!"

"Thank you," said Malik, pleased to have his wacky idea appreciated by a total stranger.

"So, Zack," said Azalea, "were those real ghosts?"

Zack laughed. "Uh, no, Azalea. That was Sammie Smith. From history class?"

"Wow. You have X-ray vision, too?"

"Nope. I recognized her voice."

"So what *do* ghosts wear on Halloween?" asked Malik, sounding genuinely interested.

"Well," said Zack, "most of the ones I've met are usually wearing what they wore when they were alive. That's one way you can tell they're, you know, not from here or now. They look old-fashioned. Like the people you see in movies."

The Ickes & Son Hardware store windows were illuminated by an impressive display of a dozen or more carved jack-o'-lanterns. Instead of candles, the hollowed-out pumpkins were lit up by low-wattage bulbs that flashed on and off in a random sequence.

"Pretty cool," said Zack.

"Yeah," said Malik. "I bet my buddy Norman rigged it up. Oh!" He reached into his Halloween sack and pulled out the black heart puzzle. "You're sure it's okay that I let Norman borrow this?"

"Yep. I don't think Aunt Ginny wants to play with it tonight."

"Come on, you guys," said Azalea. "There's loot to be had. Let's go inside and score a few Snickers bars!"

31

Barnabas wanted one of the Ickleby ghosts to venture out of the Haddam Hill Cemetery and go into North Chester to scout it out, since none of the thirteen souls were familiar with the town.

"We need a spy," he said. "To locate the Jennings boy. He will be the one to pay for what the three women did to us!"

Eddie quickly volunteered.

"I can scope things out better than anybody else," he argued. "The last man into the tomb should be the first ghost out, because, unlike the rest of you freaky-deakies, I'm hip to the modern lingo, dig?"

"You make an excellent point, Edward," said Barnabas. "Return by midnight."

So Eddie Boy's soul drifted down the highway toward town. He tried hitching a ride, but nobody could see him.

"At night, you can will yourself to become visible to whomever you choose, even those who are not ghost seers," Barnabas had told Eddie before he set out.

So he tried that.

And totally freaked out a truck driver, who drove his rig into a ditch when he saw Eddie Boy's ghost materialize in the middle of the highway. So Eddie went back to being invisible and walked into town. It didn't take too long, maybe fifteen minutes. When you're a ghost, you move fast. Very little friction.

Since it was Halloween, kids were out everywhere, dressed up as characters Eddie didn't recognize. Back in his day, the big costumes were Casper, Kiss, and Charlie's Angels. He did see one kid dressed up as a Star Wars Stormtrooper. *Dy-no-mite.* Eddie had dug that movie back in 1977. He wondered if they had ever made a sequel.

Soon he was on Main Street.

No one could see him, because he did not wish to be seen.

He stuffed his hands into his wool peacoat and watched three "Bs" in sombreros scoot into Ickes & Son Hardware, where dozens of jack-o'-lanterns glowed in the windows.

A jet-black raven, wings outstretched, swooped down out of the darkness, then perched on a street sign.

"Haw!" it croaked.

And suddenly, Eddie recognized one of the kids going into the hardware store. The one wearing glasses.

It was the punk who had brushed up against their crypt.

It was Zack Jennings!

32

At that very same moment, up in Boston, Zack's other aunt, Francine Potter, was standing at her front door, reluctantly doling out pennies to a group of trick-or-treaters.

"Candy rots your teeth," she said as she unwrapped another roll of copper coins. "A penny saved is a penny earned."

The children who weren't wearing masks looked disappointed.

Francine Potter could not care less. She hated Halloween, a holiday that turned bratty little boys and girls into something even worse: beggars.

"That's it," she said, plinking five pennies into the last outstretched plastic bag. "Happy Halloween." There was vinegar in her voice. "Now, go home. All of you!"

The children shuffled down her front steps and rejoined their parents on the sidewalk.

"What'd you get, hon?" asked one of the mothers.

"Nothin'," said her son, a boy dressed like a turtle in karate clothes.

"That's a lie!" Francine shouted. "I gave that child money. He can use those coins to help pay for college if he ever makes it past kindergarten."

The parents all gave her dirty looks. She gave them an even dirtier one back.

"Move along. You're loitering. I'll call the police!"

The clump of candy beggars hurried up the sidewalk.

Except for one mother, who just stood there in the lamplight like an idiot.

"What's your problem?" said Francine. "Move along."

A few of the grown-ups escorting the trick-or-treaters looked back.

"Who's she yelling at now?" said one.

"I don't know," said another. "There's nobody there."

33

francine Potter clearly saw a tall woman with a mop of curly hair standing beside the lamppost where the sidewalk met the pathway up to her stoop.

The woman appeared to be in her twenties and was wearing a long, flouncy dress that fluttered in the breeze.

"Why are you standing there gawking at me?" Francine demanded.

The curly-haired woman drifted closer.

"Hello, Francine."

"What? Do I know you?"

"Of course you do, Franny."

"What did you call me?"

"Franny."

"Nobody calls me that. Not since my sister . . ."

The curly-haired woman nodded slowly.

Francine Potter took one step backward. "No. My sister is dead. . . ."

The woman gave her another eerie nod.

"Susan?"

"Hello, Franny."

"Ha! That's impossible. When was your hair curly like that?"

"When I was happy. When I was an actress at the Hanging Hill Playhouse."

"Acting was a foolish waste of your time and education. Father and Mother both said so."

"Acting made me happy."

"Well, Susan, none of us are put on this earth to be happy. We are put here to do our jobs."

Francine couldn't believe she was having this conversation.

"Who are you? Why are you pretending to be my dead sister?"

"I'm not pretending."

"Impossible."

"Everything is possible on Halloween."

"No. You are not my sister."

"Yes. I am. I need you, Francine."

"What?"

"I need your body."

"What? Go away. And next Halloween put together a better costume. You don't even look the way my sister did when she died."

"You mean like this?"

In a horrifying flash, the curly-haired woman shriveled into a withered husk of ashen flesh and bone. Her paper-thin skin shrank tight against her jagged face. The mop of curly hair wormed its way down into her scalp.

It was truly her sister. Susan Potter Jennings. The way she had looked when she died.

"We are flesh of the same flesh," gasped the hideous creature. "Blood of the same blood."

Francine stumbled backward into her house. Slammed the door shut.

Suddenly, her body was wracked with spasms of pain.

A voice echoed inside her head: *"I have unfinished business with Zachary."*

Francine slumped to the carpeted floor. Her mind and memories swirled down a darkening sinkhole toward oblivion.

Zack's mother was alive again.

34

Norman Ickes was stuck behind the front counter of his father's stupid hardware store, handing out stupid candy bars to stupid kids in stupid costumes.

A very pretty girl his own age stood behind the clump of children. She was costumed in a black hooded cape, like a witch or a wizard.

"Um, d-do you want a candy bar?" Norman stammered. The girl had kinky blond hair and piercing green eyes.

"No," she said, her voice husky. "I want you."

Norman started to perspire. "Uh, excuse me?"

"I find I am strangely attracted to you . . ." She paused. "Norman Ickes."

She sounded like one of those prerecorded messages that fill in a blank with your name. Norman didn't care. No girl as pretty as this one had ever showed him even this much attention.

She pushed forward, leaned on the counter. Her hair smelled like vanilla ice cream.

"I sense that you and I are soul mates, Norman," she whispered.

"Really?" Norman blinked. Slid his aviator-frame glasses up the bridge of his nose.

"Yes. A little birdie told me where to find you."

Norman dabbed his sweaty forehead with the tip of his necktie. All of a sudden, he loved birds, wanted to study ornithology, maybe rescue a pelican.

"What time do you get off work?" the girl asked.

"Tonight?"

"Yes. Tonight. Halloween."

"Uh, about seven. Seven-thirty. My dad put me in charge of the candy."

"Your father is a coward. Afraid to embrace his destiny."

"Well, I wouldn't call him a—"

"I would. The bird told me all about him, too."

"Oh-kay."

"I'll wait for you. Outside."

"Huh?"

"When you are finished here, you and I are going for a ride."

"Really?"

"Yes. I need to take you up to the graveyard. Haddam Hill Cemetery."

"Really?" Cemetery Road on Haddam Hill was North Chester's "lovers' lane," the spot where all the high school and college kids went.

Norman tried not to let his nervousness show. He

pretended he was smooth and suave. He leaned on the counter to gaze into the witch girl's dreamy green eyes. "You want to take me up to Cemetery Road? On our first date?"

She nodded. "Yes, Norman. Everybody will be waiting."

"Oh. Is it a party?"

Her smile broadened. "Yes. A Halloween party hosted by the Icklebys."

A new group of kids rushed up to the counter.

"Trick or treat!"

"I'll wait outside," said the girl, moving toward the door as Norman robotically dished out the candy bars.

"Wait a second," he called out. "I don't know your name."

"Jenny."

"Cool. Oh, by the way, Jenny, I love your costume! It's very . . . bewitching."

She smiled and Norman could already tell: This was going to be the most amazing night of his life!

35

"Trick or treat, Norman!"

It was young Malik Sherman with two friends. And a dog. The kids were dressed up like the letter "B." The dog kept wagging its tail and scooted under the counter to sniff Norman's shoes.

He probably should've put on clean socks that morning.

"Don't worry," said one of Malik's friends, a kid wearing glasses. "Zipper is very friendly."

The dog gave the toe of his right shoe a double snort, whimpered a little, and trotted back to stand beside his owner.

"Neat costumes," Norman said to Malik. "Are you guys characters from *Sesame Street* or something?"

"No," said Malik. "We be the killer bees!"

"*Sí*, senor!" said the skinny "B" wearing glasses.

"Give us candy or we'll sting you!" said the girl.

The dog growled.

"Here you go, guys." Norman held up the plastic

pumpkin bowl filled with candy bars. "Take as many as you want."

"I think two will do," said Malik, reaching into the bowl. "We want to make sure you have enough for those who come after us."

The other two kids, the girl and the skinny one, did the same thing: They carefully selected two each. The dog just stood there, wagging his tail.

"Oh, Norman," said Malik. "I brought this for you. Thought you might find it challenging." He reached into his candy sack and pulled out a shiny black stone sculpted into the shape of a heart. "It's a 3-D interlocking puzzle."

"Interesting," said Norman, even though he was much more interested in the mysterious Jenny waiting for him out on the sidewalk.

Malik handed him the black stone heart.

"Once you pry it apart, you'll find a tiny black heart in the center of the black stone."

"We think it's onyx," said the girl. "That's a gemstone."

"Great," said Norman distractedly. "Can I keep it for a while? I'm kind of busy tonight."

"Um, I guess so," said the "B" with the glasses.

"This is my friend Zack," said Malik. "Zack Jennings. The black heart stone belongs to his aunt."

"Tell her thanks," said Norman as he slid the hefty heart into a side pocket of his cargo pants.

He'd play with it later.

After the Halloween party with Jenny and the Icklebys, whoever the heck they were.

36

Zack sensed that Malik's friend Norman was nervous about something.

He had beads of sweat all over his shiny forehead.

"Hey, Norman?" A man with a shaved head and a tiny triangle beard on his chin stomped up to the counter. "Your father just called, said I could take the night off, seeing how it's Halloween and I have a party to go to and you don't because you're such a loser so who'd invite you to their Halloween party except a bunch of even bigger losers?"

When the big guy stopped to snort some wet snot up his snout, Zack thought he looked and sounded like a college-aged version of Kurt and Kyle Snertz, the two bullies at his middle school (one of whom was now actually a friend of Zack's).

"W-well, um," stammered Norman Ickes, kind of cowering behind the cash register. "Okay, Steve. Have fun."

"Don't worry. I will." He leaned down and yanked an extension cord out of its wall socket. "Your blinking jack-o'-lanterns are blinking stupid. I told your old man they're a waste of electricity. He agreed. Happy Halloween, loser!"

Laughing, the big jerk strode out the front door as some new trick-or-treaters came pouring in. They were all wearing very cool costumes but Zack's eyes were riveted on the man who came in right behind them.

He had an old-school mullet haircut and was wearing a dark-blue peacoat with the collar turned up, like tough guys used to do in movies.

He also walked straight through a gum ball machine.

Because ghosts can do that sort of thing.

"Hello, Jennings," the guy sneered. "Pleased to meet ya, you little cheese weasel."

Zipper growled.

"Who are you?" asked Zack.

"Uh-oh," said Malik.

"Um, Zack? Who are you talking to?" asked Azalea.

He pointed toward the gum ball machine.

"Do we have a live one?" whispered Azalea.

"Actually," Zack whispered back, "it's a dead one. Judging by his hair and clothes, I'm guessing he died some-time in the seventies."

"What's he want?" said Malik.

Zack shrugged. "Don't know."

"Well, ask him," suggested Azalea.

"What do you want?"

"You, kid. Your family and mine? We got a score to settle."

The ghost strolled closer, jabbed a thumb over his shoulder.

"Course, I couldn't come at you earlier, not with all them jack-o'-lanterns glowing in the window. Those things ward off ghosts, man. But now, guess what? They're all dark and you're all mine!"

37

The ghost dude with the bad hairdo struck a kung fu pose.

"Your family has dishonored mine, Jennings!"

Zack rolled his eyes. In his experience, ghosts, no matter how much they threatened you, couldn't really do anything to hurt you; they could only scare you into doing something stupid to hurt yourself.

But then again, tonight was Halloween. The regular rules might be suspended for the ghost world's big night on the town.

"Hi-YA!" The guy jumped into a sideways flying kick.

To be safe, Zack shoved Azalea and Malik out of harm's way. "Watch out!"

Good thing he did. Karate man knocked over a whole display of saw blades, hammers, and screwdrivers. Hardware clattered across the floor. Zipper yelped and skittered sideways to avoid getting stabbed.

Oh, yeah. The rules were definitely different on Halloween.

"Hey!" shouted Norman Ickes from behind the cash register. "What's going on?"

"Uh, sorry," said Malik. "I bumped into this display. . . ."

"I'm gonna cream your two little friends, Jennings!" boasted the ghost. "And the dog? He's dead meat!" He leapt into another flying kick.

"You guys!" Zack shouted. "On your left! Paint!"

Azalea and Malik jumped out of the way just as the ghost hit a rack stacked with paint cans.

Six shelves loaded with gallon buckets came tumbling down. A couple of lids popped open. Paint splashed across the floorboards.

"Hey! Why are you guys trashing my dad's store?" shouted Norman Ickes. "I gave you candy bars!"

"It's not us," said Malik. "Honest. It's . . ."

"An earthquake!" shouted Azalea. "Everybody out! Earthquake!"

Kids screamed. Norman screamed. Then, in a panic, everybody except Malik, Azalea, and Zack streamed, screaming, out onto the sidewalk.

"Go, you guys!" Zack said.

"You sure?" asked Azalea.

"Go to the van! Zip? Get help!"

Azalea, Malik, and a snarling Zipper bolted out the door.

"Far out," said the ghost. "Just you and me, kid. Ickleby versus Jennings. Can you dig it?"

They circled each other.

"Who are you?"

"Your worst nightmare," said Mullet Man with a sneer.

Zack backed up a few steps and realized he was standing in the worst possible place—right underneath a Peg-Board loaded with box cutters, knives, and scissors, all with their blades pointed down!

"Cool it, Eddie Boy," warbled a familiar voice from the door.

It was Aunt Ginny, in her purple tracksuit, a white tube clenched in her fist. Beyond her, Zack could see his dad, Malik, Azalea, and Zipper out on the sidewalk.

"You!" said Eddie Boy Ickleby. "Where are your two grody sisters, you old hag?"

"At home, Edward. Packing flares just like this one." She popped a plastic cap off the white stick. Struck it against the doorframe. Sparks sizzled. Smoke spewed. Aunt Ginny tossed the smoldering stick at the ghost's feet.

"No!" The ghost sounded stunned. He stood stock-still, frozen in place.

"Aunt Ginny?" shouted Zack's dad from outside. "Is that a stink bomb?"

"No, Georgie. It's a smudge stick. Garlic, clove, thistle, peppermint, and of course sage. Lots and lots of sage."

"Hate . . . sage," gasped the petrified ghost. "Can't . . . move . . ."

"Yep," said Aunt Ginny. "Breathe it and weep."

Thick white clouds billowed up out of the sizzling tube.

"You . . . wretched . . . old . . . witch!" The ghost choked as he clutched his throat. He seemed to be fading. Zack could see clear through him, like the ghosts in cartoons.

"What's going on in there?" cried Zack's dad.

"Just dealing with a nasty troublemaker from 1979."

"What? Who's in there besides Zack?"

"Nobody, dear," said Aunt Ginny, moving closer to the gasping ghost. "Not for long, anyway."

Aunt Ginny bent forward and spoke directly into the dematerializing man's ear.

"It is time for you to leave. All is well. There is nothing here for you now."

The ghost's eyes went wide as he fought against the incantation.

"Go now, Edward. Complete your passing."

And with one last whimper, the ghost vanished.

Zack looked at Aunt Ginny, his eyes filled with awe and amazement.

"Wow. That was incredible."

"Is the ghost gone?" asked Azalea from the door.

"Yes, dear," said Aunt Ginny as she briskly swiped her hands clean a few times. "One down. Eleven to go."

38

"Is Zack okay?"

Judy, at George's suggestion, had put the phone on speaker. George's aunts Hannah and Sophie were standing in the front hallway, mouths hanging open, listening.

"Zack's fine," said George. "Malik and Azalea, too. According to Aunt Ginny, it was one of the Ickleby ghosts."

The two elderly aunts gasped.

"What's an Ickleby ghost?" Judy asked.

"I'm not sure," said George. "Aunt Ginny said she'd tell me more once we make certain Zack and his friends are safe and take care of the mess we made here at the hardware store. Oh, she did mention that there are eleven more of these 'evil Icklebys.'"

"Eleven more?"

Now the two elderly sisters were nodding. Sophie was also nervously nibbling on a bite-sized Baby Ruth.

"Hang on, hon," said George. "Aunt Ginny wants to talk to you."

"Okay."

"Judy? Am I on speakerphone, dear?"

"Yes, Aunt Ginny. What happened?"

"Oh, we just had an unfortunate incident. Everything's fine now, just fine. Hannah and Sophie? I packed some extra sage candles in my trunk. Maybe you two should run upstairs and retrieve a few."

"Sage candles?" asked Judy.

Judy saw Hannah and Sophie exchange worried glances.

"Well, dear," said Ginny on the phone, "they're actually more like portable smudge pots, if you will."

"They stun evil spirits into submission," said Hannah, sounding upset. "Come along, Sophie. It seems our baby sister has been up to some sort of mischief." Hannah started trudging up the staircase to the second floor.

Sophie looked at Judy. Fear filled her eyes. "Will you be giving away *all* of the Butterfinger bars?"

"Sophia?" shouted Hannah from the steps.

"Coming." Sophie followed Hannah up to the second floor.

Right after Judy slipped her a Butterfinger.

The doorbell rang as a new group of kids stormed up the front porch steps and screamed, "Trick or treat!"

Judy just hoped they weren't little Icklebys.

39

"Trick or treat!"

"Oh, my. Look at all these goblins and ghouls. Here you go, kids." Smiling, Judy started doling out the candy bars. "Neat costume, Alistair."

"Thanks, Mrs. Jennings. I like your pumpkins." The boy gestured at the six flickering jack-o'-lanterns lined up along the porch railing.

As soon as the kids were gone and the door closed, the phone began to ring again.

"Hello?" Judy answered.

There was silence on the other end.

"Hello?"

More silence.

"George? Is that you?"

"No," replied a weak voice. "This is . . . Francine."

"Excuse me?"

"This is Zack's aunt. Francine. I'm his mother's sister."

"Oh, right. Francine. Hi."

Judy had never met the woman, but from what she had gathered from George, Francine Potter-Kressin-Venable-Greene was a very wealthy, extremely crabby, exceptionally angry middle-aged woman.

From Zack, Judy had learned that "Aunt Francine hates me even more than my mother did. She blames me for killing her sister."

All in all, Aunt Francine didn't come very highly recommended.

"Is there a number where I can call you back?" asked Judy. "We're kind of busy here tonight. . . ."

"Are you Judy? The woman who took my . . ."

There was a long pause.

". . . my sister's place?"

"Excuse me?"

"Never mind. I'm on my way."

"On your way where?"

"Tell Zack it's Halloween, so I'm coming to take care of him."

Norman Ickes's father had fired him.

"It was an earthquake," Norman had tried to explain. "A kid panicked and knocked over some display racks. We had to evacuate the store."

His father wouldn't listen.

Now Norman and the strange girl, Jenny Ballard, were sitting in her car at the dead end of the dirt road that snaked up the back of Haddam Hill.

They parked in a moonlit patch of asphalt and stared at the eerie cemetery.

After several minutes with no sound but the creak of skeletal trees dancing with the wind and an angry cat's moaning at the moon, Norman finally spoke: "My father probably wishes I had never been born."

Jenny cuddled closer. "I'm very glad you were, Norman. You are the heir to an awesome line of amazing men."

"What?"

"You, Norman, are an Ickleby!"

"I am?"

"Yeah."

"What's an Ickleby?"

"Your real name."

"Ickleby Ickes?"

"No, silly. Norman Ickleby."

"Says who?"

"The voice."

"The voice?"

"It speaks to me. In here." She tapped the side of her head. "It told me to find you, to bring you here. It told me to bring this!"

She held up a very sharp hunting knife.

"Did you steal that from my dad's store?"

She nodded.

Norman sighed. "It was in a *locked* display case!"

"I unlocked it. While your father was firing you."

"Great. You stole a very expensive hunting knife. How stupid are you? My dad's going to know it's missing."

"So?"

"He'll blame me for that, too!"

"Who cares? You were meant for greater things than hawking hardware."

"Oh, really? Like what? Polishing Steve Snertz's shaved head?"

Jenny pulled up on her door handle. "Come, Norman."

"What? Where are we going?"

"To fulfill your destiny!"

The ghosts of Barnabas Ickleby's eleven descendants gathered around him outside the family crypt.

An oily black raven sat perched on the peak of the mausoleum's gabled roof.

"They sent Eddie Boy into oblivion," reported Barnabas.

The others hissed and moaned.

"Who was it?" asked Little Paulie Ickleby, the stubby ghost of a bank-robbing thug who'd died in 1959. "Who bumped off my boy?"

"The Jennings family, of course," said Barnabas. "The boy and one of the hags who imprisoned us here."

"You sure?"

"My spy saw it all." Barnabas nodded toward the black bird roosting on the roof. "They saged him first. Then the woman spoke the words."

Little Paulie twitched, cracked his knuckles, and smoothed out his jelly roll hairdo. Eddie Boy had been one of Paulie's two sons. The other one hadn't taken up the family business: crime. Instead, Paulie's second son, Herman, had become a coward—living the straight life, peddling paintbrushes, toilet seats, and duct tape in a two-bit small town.

"Send me out next," said Paulie.

"Why?"

"I'll kill the Jennings kid. Give 'em the ol' eye-for-an-eye. They hustle my boy off into the great beyond, I send theirs to an early grave."

"Perhaps we should wait until we have a body to do our bidding," suggested Barnabas.

"No way. Tonight's Halloween. We killed that old witch's cat on Halloween, remember? Up in Great Barrington. Right before they shanghaied us down here to this Nowheresville."

"True," said Barnabas.

"Hey, we may be dead, but one night a year, we're also deadly—just so long as our souls ain't sealed up in that tomb no more. Come on. The clock's ticking here. Where do I find this Jennings punk?"

The raven swooped off the roof.

Barnabas pointed toward its inky silhouette flitting across the sky.

"Follow our winged friend," said Barnabas. "He shall lead you to the child."

Zack and his friends decided to skip the costume competition.

Their poster-board "Bs" were torn during the hardware store scuffle, and now, instead of killer bees, they looked like a squashed "D," a "P," and a "3."

"We probably wouldn't have won anyway," said Azalea. "We're looking slightly B-draggled."

Zack and Malik laughed. They were riding in the backseat with Aunt Ginny. Zipper was sound asleep in Zack's lap.

"Good thing you wore your gym clothes," said Malik, indicating Aunt Ginny's purple tracksuit. "So how come you know so much about ghosts and how to vanquish them?"

"Oh, I just listened to a lot of folklore as a child. Studied the powers of herbs. We had an older cousin up in Great Barrington who knew everything about . . . herbology." She reached over to pat Zack on the knee. "You did good in there, champ."

"Thanks."

"Azalea and I might have been seriously injured," said Malik, "if Zack hadn't pushed us out of the way like that."

Zack shrugged. "I could see what the guy was doing; you two couldn't."

"Indeed," said Malik. "You have an extremely rare and useful talent, Zack."

"I guess."

Azalea turned around to ask Aunt Ginny a question. "So how come this ghost could actually do junk like knock over shelves full of paint cans? Zack told us ghosts can't do stuff like that."

"Zack is correct," said Aunt Ginny. "Ghosts are disembodied spirits, so on most days, they cannot do much in our realm. Tonight, however, is Halloween."

"Ooh," said Malik eagerly, "do they get special superpowers every October thirty-first?"

"Something like that," said Aunt Ginny. "On Halloween, the border between this world and the next is so thin, spirits can more easily reach through the veil that separates the living from the dead."

"They can reach out and touch someone," said Azalea. "Whack 'em, too."

"Well, it's eight o'clock," said Zack's dad. "They only have four more hours to reach out and wreak havoc."

"Actually," said Aunt Ginny, "they have until sunup tomorrow."

"The sun rises at 7:22 a.m. tomorrow," said Azalea.

"It was on the front page of the newspaper this morning."

"Great," said Zack. "They've got eleven and a half hours to knock junk over."

"Or try to knock people off," added Azalea.

The van was headed west on State Route 13.

Fortunately, Zack knew they would exit before reaching the Haddam Hill Cemetery. He did not want to see who else had risen to pull a Halloween all-nighter in the boneyard.

He turned to Aunt Ginny.

"Last Friday," he whispered, "I hid behind the Ickleby crypt up in the graveyard."

"Is that so?"

"Yeah. You think maybe they're mad at me for doing that? Is that why Eddie Boy came after me tonight?"

"Doubtful, dear."

They passed the tall wrought-iron gates at the entrance to Spratling Manor, a deserted stone castle built in 1882. No one had lived on the mansion grounds since Gerda Spratling and the last resident, Mr. Rodman Willoughby, her longtime chauffeur, passed away.

And there he was. Standing in front of the vine-shrouded

gates. A ghost in a black suit and driver's cap. He waved cheerily at Zack as the van passed by. Zack gave him a tentative finger wave back.

"You know, Zack," Aunt Ginny whispered, "there is a way to be rid of your gift, if that's what you want."

"Really?" Zack whispered back.

Azalea had cranked up the radio when it started playing the theme from the movie *Ghostbusters*—enough disco noise for Zack and Aunt Ginny to chat without anyone hearing what they were chatting about.

Now Zack saw Davy Wilcox walking along the edge of the road with a fishing pole slung over his shoulder.

"Howdy, pardner!" Davy shouted with a wave.

Only Zack and Aunt Ginny heard him.

"Friend of yours?" asked Ginny.

"Yeah," said Zack, feeling all warm and fuzzy inside. "That's Davy. I met him last summer. In the crossroads."

"Well, all you have to do, if you never want to see him or an Ickleby again, is drink a special drink."

"You mean like a magical herb potion?"

"Actually, it's more like a chocolate milk shake."

"Like my dad drank?"

Aunt Ginny nodded.

"And then the ghosts would all go away?"

"Well, they'd still be there. You just wouldn't be able to see them."

Zack turned back to the window and thought about what Aunt Ginny was proposing.

Ever since he had first started seeing ghosts (and not just imagining that the ghost of his dead mother was lurking in the shadows to make him pay for making her life so miserable), Zack had wished his special talent came with a gift receipt so he could take it back and exchange it for something better, like Azalea's photographic memory.

But tonight his ghost-seeing ability had helped him save Malik and Azalea from getting creamed under a heap of falling hardware or tumbling paint cans. It helped him rescue Zipper.

Tonight his special talent really did feel like a gift because he'd been able to use it to protect his friends.

"I think I'll stick with what I've got, Aunt Ginny."

"You sure?" she asked, unable to hide her pride at hearing Zack's answer.

"For now. Yeah. I'm good."

She patted his knee again. "You certainly are."

Zack smiled and looked out his window again. In an open field, six Korean War soldiers (whom Zack had also met last summer) were greeting all sorts of other soldiers: guys from World War II, Vietnam, the Civil War, the Spanish-American War, even the American Revolution. They tapped a keg of what probably wasn't root beer and passed around frothy mugs to celebrate Memorial Day on Halloween night.

"If you change your mind . . . ," said Aunt Ginny, who was also staring out the window, admiring the rowdy army men.

"I'll let you know," said Zack.

"Don't you worry, Zack," said Aunt Ginny. "This isn't your fault. My sisters and I made this mess—years ago. It's our duty to clean it up before we leave."

Zack nodded, even though he had a funny feeling that, somehow, he'd be on the cleanup crew, too.

11

Norman followed Jenny Ballard through the grave-yard gate.

"Come on."

"Where are we going?"

"To meet your ancestors."

"Why?"

They made their way through the empty cemetery.

"What if you could show everybody in North Chester who you truly are?" Jenny asked breathlessly. "What if you could become a man to be feared?"

Norman liked the sound of that.

"And no one could give me grief or call me a nerd or make fun of me? Not Steve Snertz or those brats who tossed eggs at me tonight because I stopped handing out candy after the earthquake?"

"They wouldn't dare, Norman. Not after you become the man I know you can be!"

"Oh, yeah? And who's that?"

"You, of course. But ruled by the lionhearted souls of your ancestors."

They stopped in front of what looked like a small mildew-stained chapel made of massive stone blocks. The weathered wooden door at the front of the crypt was sealed with a lock shaped like a black heart. Norman read the name inscribed over the entrance:

ICKLEBY

He felt his pulse quicken.

He was an Ickleby. These were his ancestors.

Blood surged to every muscle in his body.

"Wouldn't you like to be one of the invincible and almighty immortals, Norman?"

Norman did not answer her.

He simply grinned.

It was after eight p.m. and nobody had rung the doorbell for half an hour, so Judy figured she'd seen her last trick-or-treaters for the night.

"We found the sage candles," said Aunt Hannah, hovering in the foyer, clutching a white tube.

"Pyewacket showed us where to look," added Aunt Sophie.

"Pyewacket?"

"Virginia's cat."

"Oh. Great," said Judy, who had no idea how a cat knew where the sage candles were stored. "Speaking of candles, I'm going outside to blow out the jack-o'-lanterns."

"Oh me, oh my!" gasped Sophie.

"Is that wise?" asked Hannah.

"Well, if I don't, they'll wilt the pumpkins. Or maybe the wind will knock them off the railing and we'll burn down the house. Again."

"But . . ."

Suddenly, there was a horrible shriek—an angry yowl followed by banging, something falling, a crash, and another yowl.

"Mister Cookiepants?" snapped Aunt Hannah. "Leave Mystic alone!"

"Mystic?" cried Aunt Sophie. "Leave your sister alone. Bad cat! Bad, bad, very bad!"

The two aunts hurried up the stairs to referee a cat-fight.

Judy went out to the porch, picked up the pumpkin lids, and blew out the candles one by one. As the wicks smoldered, she savored the scent of fresh-baked pumpkin pie.

"We should all smell so good when we die, am I right?"

A stout young man swaggered toward the porch steps. He was costumed like a character from the musical *Grease*. Slicked-back hair. White T-shirt. Blue jeans. A pack of cigarettes tucked into his rolled-up shirtsleeve. When he moved into the porch light, Judy could see that what she'd thought were the white tips of cigarettes were actually writhing maggots.

"Can I help you?" asked Judy.

"Your people vaporized my son tonight. Sent him packing."

"What?"

"You're a Jennings, right?"

"Who are you?"

"They call me Little Paulie." He reached into the

pocket of his jeans and pulled out a blunt black handle that had a silver button on its front. "Little Paulie Ickleby."

Ickleby.

The ghost Zack and Ginny had battled at the hardware store had been an Ickleby.

This Ickleby pressed the button on the black knife handle. A sharp steel blade sprang up.

"Go away," said Judy. She fumbled in her pocket for a match to relight one of the jack-o'-lanterns. Couldn't find one.

The ghost put one foot on the first step.

"Hey, don't be a wet rag. Word from the bird: If you didn't want me to drop by, you shouldn't've blown out your overgrown turnips. Jack-o'-lanterns protect you, sister. Frighten spooks away."

Okay. The folktales were true.

Little Paulie Ickleby lurched up to the second step.

"First you Jenningses drag us away from home."

He climbed the third step.

"Next you rub out Eddie Boy? My favorite son? Now all I got left is chickenhearted Herman!"

Little Paulie slashed his knife angrily to the left.

It scratched a deep scar into the porch railing.

The knife blade could do serious damage. It was real.

Because tonight is Halloween, Judy realized.

"Where's your son?" asked the ghost, his eyes narrowing to reptilian slits.

"What?"

"You people take my son; we take yours. An eye for an eye, a tooth for a tooth, a boy for a boy."

Little Paulie lunged forward.

Behind Judy, the front door flew open.

A cat hissed.

"Duck!" shouted Aunt Hannah.

"Incoming!" shouted Aunt Sophie.

The two aunts leapt onto the porch and hurled smoldering white smoke bombs at the feet of Little Paulie Ickleby.

Pyewacket, Aunt Ginny's gray-and-white cat, sprang over to swat its paws at the greaser's knees. Little Paulie froze in his tracks and dropped the switchblade knife so he could clench his throat.

"You're . . . bad . . . news!" he gasped in pain.

"Especially for you, young man," said Aunt Hannah.

The aunts leaned over the gulping specter and started to chant. "It is time for you to leave. All is well. There is nothing here for you now."

Judy could've sworn that the ghost was starting to fade away, like somebody had just unplugged him.

"Go now, Paul Ickleby," said the two aunts. "Go. Complete your passing."

With one last pitiful, choking whoop, the ghost disappeared.

And somewhere, high in a tree, a bird cawed harshly.

Zack was feeling pretty good as the van headed up
Stonebriar Road for home.

He'd hang on to his ghost-seeing gift, at least until
Halloween was over. He'd protect his friends and family.

They'd already dropped off Malik and Azalea.

"Sorry we had to cut Halloween a little short," said his
dad, turning into the driveway in front of their house.

"That's okay."

"If you like, Zack," said Aunt Ginny, "we can go to the
grocery store tomorrow. I suspect all the Halloween candy
will be half price."

He chuckled.

But then he saw Judy and his dad's other two aunts up
on the porch. All three were waving their arms over their
heads the way people do when they've just witnessed a car
wreck on the highway. Zipper shot his ears up, sensing
trouble.

"Oh, my," muttered Aunt Ginny.

Zack's dad jammed on the parking brake, jumped out of the van, and raced up to the porch. Zack and Zipper were right behind him. Aunt Ginny was bringing up the rear.

"What happened?" Zack's dad asked.

"Another one of those Ickleby ghosts," said Judy. "This one looked like he was from the 1950s."

"Aha," said Aunt Ginny after she caught her breath. "Little Paulie. The next-youngest man in the mausoleum."

"What?" said Zack's dad. "Who's Little Paulie?"

"Eddie Boy's father," said Ginny.

"Who's Eddie Boy?" asked Judy.

"The ghost Aunt Ginny smoke-bombed in the hardware store," said Zack.

"Virginia?" said Aunt Hannah, her hands on her hips. "What have you done?"

"Me? Why, nothing, sister."

"How would you explain this sudden influx of evil Icklebys?"

"We three agreed," mumbled Aunt Sophie somewhat sheepishly. "I remember. We did."

"Did you use my sage candles, sisters?" Aunt Ginny asked very sweetly.

"Yes," said Hannah. She looked like she was so mad she might turn into a smoke bomb, too.

"Wonderful," said Aunt Ginny. "Two down, ten to go."

"You seem very pleased," said Hannah.

"Me? Hardly. But now that the cats are out of the bag,

so to speak, perhaps we three should go inside and discuss this matter further?"

"What matter?" asked Judy.

"Oh, we're not to speak of it," said Sophie. "It's a triple-pinky secret."

Aunt Ginny winked at Judy. "I'll clue you in later, dear." She gestured toward the front door. "Sisters? Shall we?"

Hannah harrumphed into the house. Sophie followed her.

"Oh, Georgie?" said Aunt Ginny.

"Yes?"

"We may need to stay in town a bit longer than originally planned."

Jenny Ballard found a sharp twig and etched a five-pointed star into the blackened dirt in front of the Ickleby family crypt.

Then she surrounded her pentagram with one dozen sputtering candles.

"Stand in the center of the burning circle, Norman!" she said, her voice urgent and breathy. "Prepare to welcome your ancestors into your body."

Norman hesitated.

"This is your chance!" said Jenny. "Forever banish weak Norman from your body!"

"I can make my dad pay for never standing up for me?"

"Yes, Norman."

"And Snertz? I get to cream him, too?"

"Yes."

"And those jerks from high school?"

"Yes! All who once caused you pain shall cower in fear before you."

"And evil. Do I get to be evil? Because evil people have all the fun."

"Yes."

"Good. And will you be my girlfriend?"

"Forever and ever, Norman. You shall be the evil king. I shall be your wicked queen!"

Norman boldly stepped over the flickering candles to stand in the center of the pentagram. "Let's do this thing!"

Jenny handed him a sheet of paper.

"The raven-throated voice spoke these words unto me. Recite them, Norman, and all will be as it should."

He stared at the words. They seemed to be seared onto the page.

"Ancestors, hear me!" Norman's voice grew stronger and steadier. "I praise you for the courage and cunning you showed while alive. Now, through the mists of time and the thinning veil of death, I invite you in. Take my body and use it as you see fit. Remove my cowardly soul and replace it with brazen hatred for all the weaklings of this world!"

He dropped the script. He didn't need it anymore.

"I, Norman Ickleby, no longer have any desire to use this body for my own purposes. Take it. Take me. Take me now!"

At that instant, thunder clapped and a leaf-swirling wind blew out the circle of twelve candles.

The man who used to be Norman Ickes slumped to the ground, an empty vessel longing to be filled.

Barnabas and the other ten remaining Ickleby souls surrounded the pentagram, each man standing where an unlit candle stood.

They stared down at the quivering body of their heir, Norman Ickleby.

They made the witchy woman feel an icy prickle of fear and foreboding up her spine.

"Let me enter the body!" demanded Cornelius, the notorious embezzler.

"Fie upon it," cried Silas, who in 1789 had been executed for treason. "I have suffered in this interminable limbo far longer than he!"

"I want to live again!" whined Rilke, the mass-murdering scoundrel.

"Silence," rasped Barnabas. "I have made my decision. Isador? Enter this newfound flesh."

"Sure, sure," said Crazy Izzy, the gangster from the 1930s. "I'll give little Zack Jennings the big kiss-off. I'll bump off his mutt, too!"

"Go! Steal Norman's body! Use him to do all the things I command you to do!"

Crazy Izzy transmogrified into a throbbing ball of searing ultraviolet light.

"I get first dibs 'cause them Jennings bumped off my son and my grandson—Little Paulie and Eddie Boy. Right?"

"No," said Barnabas, his eyes burning brightly inside the slits of his mask. "You are given this chance simply because you, like I, have no qualms about killing children."

Crazy Izzy's soul shot across the threshold between the living and the dead.

He took over the body of Norman Ickes.

"Did Aunt Ginny give you any clue as to what the heck's going on?" Judy asked as she tucked Zack in for the night down in the rumpus room.

"Not really," said Zack. "Just that the ghost downtown was an Ickleby and that Ginny and her sisters will take care of everything before they leave."

Zipper, who was curled up near Zack's knees, wagged his tail, happy to hear that the elderly aunts would be leaving. He hoped the cats would be leaving, too!

"But it sounds like the worst will be over by tomorrow morning," Zack continued. "I think everybody has to be back in their coffins by sunrise."

"Good," said Judy. "Oh, I almost forgot."

"What?"

"While you guys were downtown, your aunt Francine called."

Zack sank about three inches under the covers. "Really?"

"She said she wanted to come see you."

"What'd you tell her?"

"That this wasn't a very good time."

"Excellent! Thanks."

"You and your dad never liked her, huh?"

"Nope. I think Aunt Francine hates me even more than my mother did. Blames me for killing her sister."

"Which you didn't do, Zack."

"I know that. But, Judy?"

"Yeah?"

"Aunt Francine doesn't. At the funeral, when nobody else was around, she said, 'This is all your fault.'"

"That's horrible."

Zack shrugged. "By then, I was sort of used to it. Whenever Aunt Francine would visit, she and my mom would sit in the dining room and smoke cigarettes and tell each other what a rotten kid I was."

"Zack, I am so sorry. . . ."

"Yeah. Me too." Zack took in a deep, steadying breath. "But that was then and this is now. I just don't want Aunt Francine bringing too much 'then' up here to mess with my great new 'now.'"

"Tell you what," said Judy. "If she calls again, I'll just tell her there's no room at the inn." She leaned down and kissed Zack on his forehead. "I'll deal with Aunt Francine. You stick to the ghosts."

"Deal."

"Sleep well, honey."

"Will do."

Zack pulled a sage candle out from under his pillow.

"What's that?" asked Judy.

"My little friend," said Zack, doing his killer bee accent. "Aunt Ginny gave it to me when she came down to tuck me in."

"So you've been double-tucked?"

"Yeah."

"Good. You deserve it."

"Oh, shoot," said Zack.

"What?"

"I meant to tell Aunt Ginny that Malik loaned her puzzle to a friend."

"Huh?"

"We found this brainteaser in her trunk and Malik asked me if his friend could borrow it. I said yes. I was going to tell Aunt Ginny but things got so busy, first in the hardware store, then here, I just forgot!"

"You found this puzzle in her trunk? The trunk that seems to have exploded all over your bedroom?"

"Yeah."

"Don't worry. I don't think Aunt Ginny will mind. Trust me—she still has plenty of other toys to play with."

Zack smiled. "Okay. Thanks, Mom."

"See you in the morning, hon."

She flicked off the lights and shut the door.

Zack closed his eyes and, wiped out from the most exciting and most exhausting Halloween he could remember, started drifting off to sleep.

Around midnight, Zack heard Zipper panting.

Really loudly.

And the wet dribble of dog drool.

Actually, it couldn't be Zipper. The panting was too heavy and Zipper seldom slobbered.

Zack opened an eye.

Grandpa Jim was sitting in his favorite chair again. This time, he had brought along the big black dog with the glowing red eyeballs.

"Rest up, Zack," he said, patting the dog on its massive head. "Shuck and I will keep our eyes peeled for any trouble."

"Is it coming?"

"Most likely. I have a feeling this thing will get worse before it gets any better."

51

Jenny Ballard watched Norman Ickes twitching on the ground, his kicking feet knocking down the dead candles.

"Norman?" She bent down to touch his cold and clammy forehead. "Norman?"

He wasn't breathing.

"Ohmigod. Norman? Norman!"

An eye popped open.

Jenny put a hand over her racing heart.

"You scared me. I thought you were dead."

Norman's head and torso bolted upright into a sitting position. He sucked down a deep breath.

"That's it, Norman," said Jenny. "Breathe. Nice and easy."

A smirk curled Norman's lip. "What's your name again?"

"Jenny. Remember?"

Norman stood up. His legs seemed kind of rubbery as he dusted off his pants. "Sure, sure. Jenny. You're the dame Barnabas has been bossin' around."

"Excuse me?"

"What's this?" Norman, more uncoordinated than usual, dug into his pocket and pulled out a black stone shaped like a heart. "Well, ring-a-ding-ding. Your Norman was a swell egg. Scamming the charm off the witches? That's smooth."

"Huh?"

"This here's the warden's key, toots." The man who looked like Norman tossed the shiny stone up and caught it as if it were a black apple. "So, did you bring the knife?"

"Yes, Norman. I did everything the raven voice told me to do."

"Atta girl. Fork it over."

Jenny handed the weapon, which had a curved blade on the bottom and jagged saw teeth on the top, to the man who really wasn't Norman anymore.

"Who are you?" she asked. "Are you one of Norman's deceased ancestors?"

"That's right. My friends used to call me Izzy. Crazy Izzy Ickleby."

"When did you die?"

"About seventy years before you."

"What? I'm not—"

Before Jenny could say "dead," the man who used to be Norman jammed the knife blade into her stomach and twisted it sharply to the right.

"Say hello to all my pals on the other side, toots."

And those were the last words Jenny Ballard ever heard.

146

Around ten, Judy sat down in the breakfast nook with a second cup of coffee and breathed a sigh of relief.

It was the morning after Halloween. Zack and the whole family had survived. Yes, there would be some expenses related to the damages at Ickes & Son Hardware and they'd need to fix up the porch railing where it had been scarred by a ghost's extremely lethal knife, but all in all, things could have been worse.

Now it was November 1, the sun was shining, George had gone down to New York City on the 7:10 train, Zack had taken the bus to school, and Judy had the house to herself. Well, except for George's three aunts, who seemed to be sleeping in.

Zipper sank into his doggy bed and let out his own long sigh. Poor guy looked bushed.

"Relax, Zip," said Judy. "Halloween is officially over."

That was when George's three aunts bustled through the kitchen, making a beeline for the back door.

"Good morning, Judy," chirped Aunt Ginny as she bobbled by.

Aunt Hannah and Aunt Sophie were right behind her.

"Good morning, ladies," said Judy. "Hey, I was wondering—should we talk some more about last night and all these Icklebys?"

"We were wondering the same thing," huffed Aunt Hannah. "Sisters? Outside. Now!"

"Can I come with you?"

"Sorry, dear," said Aunt Sophie. "It's not a good idea."

"Huh?"

"Enjoy your coffee, dear," said Aunt Ginny. "We really don't have anything to talk about besides this lovely weather. . . ."

"Oh, yes we do, Virginia!" said Hannah.

The three sisters, trailed by their three cats, scuttled out the back door.

Judy gave the ladies a few seconds and then slipped over to the sink so she could spy on them through the curtains.

The three of them were standing in a circle around the kettle-shaped barbecue grill.

"Perhaps we should eat breakfast first?" said Aunt Sophie.

"No," fumed Aunt Hannah. "Virginia, you did this, didn't you?"

"I did not!" said Ginny. "But now that they're out, we need to act swiftly. I think we should—"

Suddenly, Ginny glanced at the kitchen window.

Judy hurriedly retreated from the sink, returned to the breakfast nook, and snapped on the countertop TV so she could pretend that was what she'd been doing all along if Aunt Ginny came back in.

"And in local news," said the television anchorwoman, "police suspect foul play in the Haddam Hill Cemetery outside North Chester, where, late last night, some local teenagers discovered the body of Ms. Jenny Ballard. Dressed in what the police described as a 'witch's robe,' the young girl may have been murdered in what authorities speculate was a bizarre Halloween ritual."

The TV showed the crime scene marked off by police tape in front of a mausoleum. A name was chiseled over the door:

ICKLEBY

Ickleby!

Who were these people?

Judy gulped one last swig of coffee. "Zip, guard the house. I need to run to the library—now."

53

Crazy Izzy Ickleby walked up the main drag of North Chester inside Norman Ickes's body.

His new skin suit didn't quite fit right, so his feet kept slip-sliding sideways, like he was walking around in socks on a just-waxed wood floor. Izzy didn't care if he looked like a loose-limbed palooka. He had a body. He was breathing again. He was alive!

And he had a job to do for the big cheese, Barnabas.

He needed to get hold of a gun and some money.

Fortunately, while shoving Norman's soul out of the driver's seat, Izzy was able to tap into the sap's memory banks. He now knew everything Norman had ever known, including all sorts of useless bunk about solving puzzles and the different sizes of crescent wrenches.

He also knew where Norman's coworker, Stephen Snertz, stashed his heater—a six-shot Smith & Wesson.

Izzy walked Norman up the sidewalk to the hardware

store. Some jingle-brained mug was on a ladder, painting over "Son" in the Ickes & Son Hardware sign.

"That's Snertz! Stephen Snertz!" said whatever bit of Norman was still awake inside his brain. *"Kill him! Kill Snertz!"*

"Later," Crazy Izzy thought back. *"I promise."*

"Hiya, Steve," he had Norman say out loud, just to sound sociable-like.

"Norman? What are you doing here, you idiot? You're fired."

"Yeah. Thanks for reminding me, pal."

Izzy gave the ladder a swift kick.

Snertz and his paint bucket went *splat* all over the concrete. The big lug wasn't dead, just conked out. Of course, he wouldn't be dancing no time soon, neither.

"Ooh, that felt good!" sighed the Norman inside Izzy's head. *"Real good."*

"Don't worry, kid," Izzy thought back. *"That's just the start of what we're gonna do to that big lug."*

Whistling nonchalantly, he had Norman amble into the hardware store, hop over the counter, and grab Snertz's pistol, which was stashed on a shelf with a box of bullets. Since no one was looking, Izzy popped open the cash register and pocketed a couple hundred clams, too.

"Can we go shoot Snertz now?" asked the Norman voice.

"Not yet, kid. First we need to stash the black heart stone, hide it someplace safe where no one can find it."

Fortunately, the raven had told Barnabas exactly where Izzy should squirrel the rock. And if anybody tried to tag along to see where he ditched the stone, he'd drill 'em full of lead.

Because, thanks to Norman, trigger-happy Izzy had a brand-new trigger finger.

Most sixth graders would probably consider a class field trip to the town library kind of dull, but Zack couldn't have been more excited.

He wanted to ask the town librarian, Mrs. Jeanette Emerson, a few questions about this Ickleby clan—the family who seemed to have some kind of feud going against the Jennings family.

Zack, Malik, and Azalea climbed aboard the big yellow bus waiting for them in the parking lot of Pettimore Middle School.

"Hello, again!" said the smiling lady behind the big steering wheel. "How are my three musketeers?"

"Just fine, Ms. Tiedeman," said Zack.

The bus driver, Ms. A. J. Tiedeman, picked up Zack, Azalea, and Malik at their bus stops every morning and brought them home every afternoon. She always drove the school bus safely but she also knew how to make all sorts of tire-screeching evasive moves in case she had to—like she was a stunt double in an action movie. Fortunately, she was also one of the first owner-drivers to install three-point seat belts on her bus. One rumor had it that before moving to North Chester, Ms. Tiedeman had raced tweaked-out trucks around mud tracks in Mississippi. Another said she was the original driver of Bigfoot's Panic Attack, the top truck from the Monster Jam that played big-city arenas all across the country.

Whatever her background, A. J. Tiedeman—who always wore leather driving gloves, wraparound shades, and a jumpsuit with flames on the shoulders and a sequined "A. J." splashed across the back—was the coolest school bus driver Zack had ever met.

She cranked shut the door after the substitute history teacher, Mrs. Chang, climbed aboard.

"Buckle up, everybody," she said to her huge horizontal rearview mirror as she goosed the gas pedal a few times, making the bus rumble and roar. Zack often wondered if A. J. Tiedeman had replaced the original school bus motor with the engine from Bigfoot's Panic Attack.

"Good morning, everybody," said the librarian, Mrs. Emerson, when Zack's history class entered the quaint old building. "My assistant, Ms. Sharon Rawlins, will give you a tour of our historic facility. But remember: A library is not a shrine for the worship of books. It's a place where history and ideas come to life!"

While the rest of the class followed Ms. Rawlins over to a big stained glass window, Zack slipped away from the pack to talk to Mrs. Emerson, who had wiry white hair and wore purple reading glasses—not to mention funky sweaters with junk like pumpkins or autumn leaves knit all over them—and was always saying stuff like that thing about libraries. It was why Zack and Judy both thought she was pretty cool.

"Mrs. Emerson?"

"Yes, Zack?"

"I need your help."

"Well, dear, that's why I'm here."

"I need to learn about the Ickleby family."

"The ones up in the Haddam Hill Cemetery?"

"Yeah. Those guys."

"Right this way. I've already pulled everything we have on the subject."

Wow. Mrs. Emerson was some kind of super librarian. She knew the answers to Zack's questions before he even asked them!

"Mrs. Chang?" she called out to Zack's teacher. "Zachary and I will be in my office working on a history project."

"Oh," said Mrs. Chang. "But he'll miss the tour."

"That's okay," said Zack. "I'm a regular here."

Mrs. Emerson led Zack around a cluster of reading tables.

"Quite the crime family, these Icklebys," said Mrs. Emerson. "One was a bank robber and another was a miner who stole other miners' gold. There was even a gangster whom Al Capone himself nicknamed Crazy Izzy Ickleby."

"Wow."

"On the other hand, the very first Ickleby to come to America, Squire Barnabas Ickleby, was revered as a pillar of his community. He even helped the early colonists erect a lovely church in the Berkshire Mountains."

"So Barnabas was a good guy?"

"Apparently so. But his son, Lucius? Robbed his neighbors and killed their cows. You can read all about his trial for capital crimes in the Boston newspapers from the 1760s."

"Mrs. Emerson?"

"Yes, Zack?"

"Boston and the Berkshires are both in Massachusetts, right?"

"Indeed they are."

"So the Icklebys aren't from North Chester or even Connecticut?"

"That's right."

"Well, why isn't the family crypt back in the Berkshires at that church the good guy helped build? Didn't they have a graveyard?"

"Aha. You Jenningses all think alike."

"Huh?"

Mrs. Emerson pushed open the door to her office.

Judy was seated at the desk.

"Your stepmother just asked me the very same question!"

"Shouldn't you be out there with the rest of your class?" Judy asked Zack.

"Why should he be out there when the answers he seeks are in here?" said Mrs. Emerson.

Judy smiled. "You're right. Come on, Zack. Let's figure this thing out."

Judy swiveled around to clack a computer keyboard.

"I was just doing an Internet search on 'Ickleby family crypt.' I think I found the connection."

"The connection to what, dear?" asked Mrs. Emerson, peering over her reading glasses at the computer screen.

"How the Jenningses and the Icklebys are related."

"Oh, my. Your husband's family is related to these nefarious miscreants?"

"No. Look at this: In 1979, right after the funeral for Edward Ickleby . . ."

Judy scrolled down through the newspaper article. A picture popped up of a nasty-looking man with a mullet haircut.

"That's him!" said Zack. "Eddie Boy! The guy Aunt Ginny and I had to, you know, take care of on Halloween night."

"I take it this Eddie Boy was a ghost?" said Mrs. Emerson.

"Yeah," said Zack. Mrs. Emerson was a big believer in supernatural stuff, so it was okay to tell her the truth. "He looked just like that picture until Aunt Ginny stunned him with the sage stink bomb and started chanting at him. Then he disappeared."

"Interesting. The Native Americans often used white sage in a sacred smoke bowl blessing to dispel evil spirits from their midst. I see that the Jennings sisters are still dabbling in spiritual herbology."

"Did you know them?" asked Judy. "When they lived here in North Chester?"

"Not very well. They are, after all, several years older than me. But one did hear stories."

"What kind?" said Zack.

"Oh, several of the local gossips claimed that the Jennings sisters were, well . . . *different*. They were known to dabble in herbs and potions. Spent a good deal of time at the Hedge Pig Emporium on Main Street, where they sell all manner of nontraditional remedies."

"They also make a mean milk shake," said Zack.

"Indeed? Never heard that."

"Aunt Ginny told me."

"I see. She's quite a character, your great-aunt. They say in her youth, Virginia Jennings would spend many nights out in the woods, talking to owls and raccoons—communing with their spirits. She and her two sisters, Sophie and Hannah, liked to dance in the misty meadow out near Spratling Manor whenever the moon was full. I am told they danced au naturel."

"Excuse me?" said Zack.

"They would dance about naked."

Zack closed his eyes and tried not to think about what that might've looked like.

"And of course," said Mrs. Emerson, "none of the Jennings girls was ever without a cat or two. One of which was always black."

"Did people say they were witches?" blurted Zack. "Because that's what I think. When Aunt Ginny did the sage deal and started chanting at the ghost, that's when I said, 'Yep, Dad's aunt is a witch.'"

He heaved a sigh of relief. He was glad he'd finally said it out loud.

"Oh-kay," said Judy, "let's just say George's aunts are a bit peculiar. Here's how the Jenningses and the Icklebys get all tangled up together."

She clicked the computer mouse and brought up the next page of the newspaper article.

Zack just prayed it wasn't a story about naked moon dancing.

"It's a pretty short article," said Judy. "Just a three-paragraph notice in the 'Goings-On About Town' column."

Mrs. Emerson leaned in to examine the screen more closely.

"Well, what exactly was going on, dear?" she asked.

Judy read from the newspaper report. "'Immediately after the funeral for convicted felon Edward "Eddie Boy" Ickleby at Saint Barnabas Episcopal Church in Great Barrington, Massachusetts, all thirteen coffins in the Ickleby family's ancestral mausoleum were removed from the family crypt and transported forty miles south by truck to North Chester, Connecticut.'"

"Why?" asked Mrs. Emerson.

"The newspaper doesn't really say. It just reports that all thirteen Ickleby men 'who had been interred' in the crypt behind Saint Barnabas church, which was founded by Squire Barnabas Ickleby and other 'good Christian men' in the early 1700s, would 'find their eternal rest in an empty mausoleum down in Connecticut's Haddam Hill Cemetery.' It also mentions that 'counting the recently deceased Edward Ickleby, twelve of the thirteen coffins removed from the ancient tomb contained the remains of Ickleby men who had been convicted of committing heinous crimes against their fellow man' and that the transfer would be 'supervised by the sheriff of North Chester Township, James Jennings."

"Grandpa?" said Zack.

"Yep," said Judy.

"Oh, my," said Mrs. Emerson.

And then nobody said anything for two whole minutes.

57

Thanks to Norman, Crazy Izzy was able to stash the black heart stone where nobody could ever find it.

Turned out the puzzle-cracking hardware-store clerk also knew how to pick the one lock in the one door that blocked his entrance to the hiding spot Barnabas had selected for the stone. When that job was done and Izzy came out of the building, he saw a black bird sitting on top of a parking meter.

All of a sudden, Barnabas started croaking at him inside his noggin.

"Go to Stansbury Stables. There you will find a black stallion by the name of Ebony. Steal him. Bring him to the crypt."

"What about killing the Jennings kid?" Crazy Izzy thought back, even though his brain was wracked with pain, what with Norman and Barnabas both yakking it up inside his skull.

"That task can wait."

"For what?" he shouted out loud.

"Never mind. Bring me the horse!"

"All right, already! I'll do it!"

The throbbing headache ended.

"Norman?" said a new voice. A real one. "Are you okay?" It was a goon in a cop uniform.

"That's Michael Wasicko," Norman's voice piped up inside Izzy's head. *"He was in my chess club in high school."*

"Don't worry, Mike," said Izzy out loud. "I'm fine."

"You were talking to yourself."

"Yeah. Guess I drank too much giggle juice."

"You still watching all those old movies like you used to?" said the cop. "Because you sure sound like one."

"Yeah. Sure. You still play chess?"

"Yep, but not as good as you. You sure you're okay? You look a little wobbly on your feet. Can I give you a ride somewhere?"

"Yeah, Mike. That'd be swell. I need to head over to Stansbury Stables."

"That horse ranch east of town?"

"Right. Whattaya say we take a powder, head over that way?"

The cop checked his watch.

"Sure, Norm. I get an hour for lunch. I'll drive you over."

"Swell."

"You want me to wait? Give you a lift back to town? Like I said, I get the whole hour for lunch."

"No thanks, pal. I'll just ride my horsey home."

58

Judy found Mrs. Chang and told her that Zack would have to miss school for the rest of the day.

"Is everything okay?" asked the teacher.

"Are you feeling all right, Zack?" asked Malik as the whole history class crowded around Zack and his stepmom in the main hall of the library.

"Did you eat every piece of your trick-or-treat candy last night?" said Azalea. "Does your stomach hurt?"

"No, my stomach doesn't hurt," said Zack, feeling a little defensive.

"We need to go see a priest," said Judy. "About some funeral arrangements."

"Oh, my," said Mrs. Chang.

"Who died?" asked Malik, sounding extremely concerned.

"Mr. *Ickleby*," said Zack very broadly, hoping Malik and Azalea would take the hint.

"The poor man from the earthquake?" said Azalea, mugging a wink.

"Yeah," said Zack. "Him."

"He was such a wise old *sage*," said Malik to let Zack know he understood what was going on, too.

"I'll let Zack's other teachers know he will be out for the rest of the day," said Mrs. Chang. "Please give our condolences to the family."

"Oh, we will," said Judy.

If we can find any Icklebys who are still alive, thought Zack.

While A. J. Tiedeman drove Zack's history class back to school, he and Judy would be heading north to Saint Barnabas Church in the Berkshire Mountains of Massachusetts. The current pastor, a Father Clayton Abercrombie, had been at the church since 1977. When Mrs. Emerson called, Father Abercrombie said he would be happy to meet with Zack and Judy.

"Let's run home and grab Zipper," said Judy as they climbed into their car in the library parking lot. "He needs a break from all those cats."

"Yeah," said Zack. "I think he might be allergic. To their claws, anyway."

It only took about an hour for Zack, Judy, and Zipper to drive from North Chester to the small country church. It was the middle of the afternoon but the sky was already dark under heavy clouds. The white clapboard church building was tucked into a weedy field under a webbed canopy of overgrown trees.

When they piled out of the car, Zack saw a priest dressed all in black standing outside the dilapidated church's front door.

Everything about Saint Barnabas Episcopal Church looked old. Paint was peeling off the shingles. The door had been painted red ages ago but was now the color of watery tomatoes. The roof was bowed and cracked.

Zipper tucked his tail between his legs. This eerie old church in the middle of nowhere was giving him the willies, too.

"Mrs. Jennings?"

"Yes," said Judy.

"I'm Father Clayton Abercrombie."

The Episcopal priest reminded Zack of a nervous ferret from a cartoon.

Judy reached out to shake the priest's trembling hand.

"Thanks for agreeing to meet with us," she said. "I'm Judy. This is my stepson, Zack. You met his grandfather a long time ago. Sheriff James Jennings."

The priest's left eye twitched. "Tell me—the spirits? Are they stirring again?"

Judy nodded. "Yeah. They're stirring."

"Big-time," added Zack.

Father Abercrombie bit his knuckle. "Has anyone been hurt?"

"A girl," said Judy. "She was found dead outside the Ickleby crypt in the Haddam Hill Cemetery."

The priest made a quick sign of the cross and said, "Please, follow me."

They made their way around the church building to its ancient graveyard.

"The original Ickleby crypt is in the farthest corner," said Father Abercrombie as they walked through the field of faded headstones, many of which dated back to the 1700s.

"Barnabas Ickleby was the first warden of this parish. A very generous, very munificent man. Provided all the money to erect our original building. He was, of course, initially buried here."

He gestured toward a sagging marble mausoleum.

Zack and Judy were staring at the blackened earth circling the old Ickleby crypt. It was as if someone had burned a three-foot path around the original family tomb. Dead ivy vines crept up the grime-covered walls.

"My wife and I came to this church when I was a very young man, back in 1977," said Father Abercrombie. "In no time at all, my parishioners started regaling me with ghost stories about the Icklebys. How, through the centuries, the evil ones rose up from this crypt on Halloween night to walk the earth and wreak havoc. You do know the nature of the twelve men who were buried in this vault with Barnabas?"

Judy nodded. "We have a pretty good idea."

"Most of the Icklebys, the good ones, were buried out here. You can see their headstones sprinkled in amongst the rest. But the bad ones, well—Barnabas had given the church so much gold, every priest who has ever served here was content to look the other way when it came time to entomb yet another Ickleby sinner behind the heavy doors of their family crypt."

Father Abercrombie swallowed hard.

"My turn came in 1979. The young thief the newspapers called Eddie Boy was gunned down in a convenience store robbery after slaying the owner and three teenaged customers. Several days before the funeral, I, for the first time, opened the Ickleby crypt—to make certain we had room for yet another casket."

The priest started nibbling on his knuckle again.

"Then what happened?" asked Judy.

"Days later, the evil revealed itself."

"On the morning of the funeral," the priest continued, "when next I opened the doors to the mausoleum, all of the coffins had been rearranged!"

"Did somebody sneak in and do it as a prank?" asked Zack.

"Impossible. That door is six inches thick. The lock is made of iron. Only I have the key."

The clergyman crept closer to the creepy crypt.

"I tried to ignore what I had seen, to construct a rational explanation. Perhaps there was metal in the coffins and a shift in the earth's magnetic field had caused them to slide into their unusual configuration."

Maybe there was an earthquake, thought Zack.

"When the funeral service concluded and the pallbearers carried Edward's coffin into the tomb, the caskets had moved once more! The one against the wall was upside down. Three had organized themselves into an 'I' formation. An 'I' for 'Ickleby'!"

The priest stared at the crypt doors—as if he feared they'd suddenly swing open and swallow him whole.

"Months later, on Halloween, some children reported hearing voices inside the mausoleum. That night, horrible deeds were done."

"By trick-or-treaters?" asked Zack.

"Trick-or-treating children do not burn down barns or slash the throats of innocent animals. They do not kill the one witness who survived Eddie Boy's convenience store rampage and testified against him in court."

"All this happened on Halloween night?" asked Judy.

"Yes. The following morning, I once again entered the Ickleby crypt."

"Had the coffins been rearranged again?" asked Judy.

"All thirteen were upside down and resting on their lids."

Zack's eyes went wide as he imagined it.

"I didn't know what to do," said Father Abercrombie. "I could not harbor the spirits of demons here on sacred soil!"

And so you shipped them off to us, thought Zack. *Nice.*

"With nowhere else to turn, I consulted a wise old woman who lived in a hovel deep in the woods. I had heard of her . . . reputation."

Judy said it first: "Was she a witch?"

"Some would certainly call her that. Her name, as I recall, was Harriet, and she was quite familiar with the

Icklebys and their evil ways, for she claimed a swarm of Ickleby ghosts had, on that very same Halloween night, slain her favorite pet. A black cat she called Grizzmaldo."

"When was this?" asked Judy.

"Thirty years ago. My wife—may she rest in peace—thought I had gone mad, prattling on about the ghosts of the evil Icklebys, the coffins in the crypt, decapitated cats, witchy women in the woods. . . ."

"How did this Harriet know it was Ickleby spirits who killed her cat?" Judy asked.

"She saw them. A crowd of twelve ghosts, one brandishing an axe. 'Who are you?' she demanded. 'We be Icklebys,' they replied. 'This night belongs to us and all those who would do evil even after death!' The one with the axe used it on her black cat."

Zipper moaned. He wouldn't wish that kind of cruelty on any creature, even ones with claws.

"I begged the wise woman of the woods to do something. Anything. This churchyard had to be cleansed of its foul spirits! She agreed. Said she wanted the cursed Ickleby corpses moved as far from their familiar haunts as possible. She told me she would contact certain cousins, three distant sisters who might be able to help us both."

Zack looked at Judy. They both realized who Harriet's three cousins had to be: Ginny, Sophie, and Hannah.

Now the priest stared down at Zack. "That week, all my prayers were answered. Your grandfather, Sheriff James Jennings—may God bless his soul—contacted me. He told me he wasn't sure why, but his sisters had insisted that he call to tell me about 'the empty Spratling crypt.'"

"Spratling!" mused Zack.

"A wealthy family that lived in North Chester, the town where your grandfather was sheriff."

"We know all about the Spratlings," said Judy.

"Well, apparently, they had built a family crypt in the Haddam Hill Cemetery, which they never used because they built a second, much more elaborate mausoleum on the grounds of their estate."

Zack and Judy (and probably even Zipper) could pretty much figure out what had happened next.

Grandpa Jim sent a truck and some men up to Great Barrington to empty the coffins out of the Massachusetts crypt so they could be transported forty miles south to Connecticut. The caskets were quietly loaded into the empty Spratling mausoleum in the cemetery. The heavy wooden doors were closed and locked. That was that.

"There was no service. No funeral rites," the priest continued. "They simply removed the stone inscribed with the Spratling name and replaced it with a marble slab reading 'Ickleby,' or so I am told. I have never actually visited the Haddam Hill Cemetery."

"That's why it's so white," said Zack.

"Excuse me?"

"The Ickleby name above the door. It looks newer than all the other stones."

"You've visited this mausoleum?"

Zack nodded.

"Do you know the Ickes family?" the priest asked Judy.

"No, I don't think so."

"They run the hardware store," said Zack. "Ickes and Son. On Main Street. The son is a friend of Malik's. They're in a puzzle club or something."

"They're Icklebys!" said the priest. "Good ones, but I remember fearing for them when I first heard that they had moved to North Chester. You see, the father, Herman Ickleby, now calls himself Herman Ickes. He was Eddie Boy Ickleby's brother. Herman was so ashamed of what his older brother had done that he took his pregnant wife and fled from Great Barrington. I never found the courage to tell him about the new location of the cursed Ickleby crypt. Poor Herman. He had wanted to move away from the earthly remains of his evil ancestors. Unfortunately, he ended up moving closer!"

Zack, Judy, and Zipper said goodbye to the fidgety priest, who hurried off to the rectory, the dilapidated house where he lived all by himself, and locked the door.

"So now we know how the Icklebys got down to North Chester," said Zack as they hiked up the hill to Judy's car.

"And I think all those evil Icklebys didn't want to make the move," said Judy. "They knew their way around Great Barrington. Knew where to find their enemies and how to terrorize them."

"So you think they're still mad at Dad's aunts for shipping their coffins down to North Chester?"

Judy nodded. "They only started popping up after the three sisters came to visit us."

"Guess they're mad at us now, too," said Zack, remembering the ghost who'd tried to kung fu him in the hardware store and the one who'd tried to slash Judy on the front porch with his switchblade knife.

"Well," said Judy, "we are Jenningses."

"Yeah," said Zack. "So do you want to change your name back to Judy Magruder?"

She laughed. "No thanks. Being a Jennings is much more exciting."

The stable owner, a doll all decked out in riding pants and one of them velvety chin-strap helmets, walked the big black stallion into a horse trailer hooked up to the rear bumper of a heavy-duty pickup truck.

She'd already tossed in a saddle and a bunch of what they called tack.

"You certainly know how to pick a horse, Mr. Ickes," she said to Norman, who was really Crazy Izzy Ickleby. "Ebony's bloodlines go all the way back to the first Arabian stallion brought to this continent in 1723."

The purebred horse's tail plume swished back and forth proudly as Miss Horseypants patted his glossy flanks.

"Look, doll, it's getting dark. Whattaya say we quit flappin' our gums and go into the barn there and settle up?"

"It's a paddock, sir, not a barn."

"Tomato, tomahto." Izzy reached into Norman's pocket and pulled out the wad of cash he had pinched from the hardware store.

"You intend to pay for Ebony with cash?"

"What, my lettuce is no good?"

"Well, I'm just surprised you would carry so much money on your person."

"Sure, sure. I'm lousy with dough."

"Very well. I'll write up the papers."

"Swell."

"After, of course, you give me the five hundred thousand dollars."

They closed up the horse carrier and went back into the small office at the front of the stables.

"I don't mean to be rude, sir, but might I see the rest of your cash?"

"Sure, sure."

Izzy reached down into his coat pocket. The one with the pistol packed in it. He whipped the weapon up and bashed the lady hard on the head with the butt of it.

The dizzy dame crumpled to the floor. She was out cold.

"*Ooh, that was incredible,*" said Norman's voice inside Izzy's head. "*I never knocked anybody out before. I never even punched a person.*"

"Stick around, kid. I'm just gettin' started."

Izzy dragged the unconscious dame into Ebony's empty stall, tied her up to a hitching post with a bunch of leather bridles, stuffed a wad of hay into her kisser, and gagged her tight with a cowboy-style kerchief he found hanging on a hook.

"That ought to hold her," he said when he finished binding and gagging the stable owner.

"Now can we please go kill Stephen Snertz?" Norman's voice begged inside Izzy's head.

A black raven swooped into the stables and landed on the top rail of a stall.

"Haw!" it croaked.

Izzy got the picture.

"Sorry, Norm. No can do. Snertz will have to wait. Seems Barnabas wants to go on a pony ride."

Izzy Ickleby used to drive beer trucks for the mob in Chicago.

So piloting the pickup hauling the horse trailer down the highway was no big whoop.

He was only a mile or two away from the Haddam Hill Cemetery when he felt something he hadn't felt in seventy years.

He was hungry. Starving!

It was nearly six o'clock and he hadn't eaten anything all day. His headlights hit a sign: The Hi-Way 31 Eat and Run. He gave the hash house a quick up and down. The blinking sign in the window said they served hot apple pie.

Izzy slammed on the brakes, squealed wheels, and pulled his rig into the parking lot.

"Wait out here," he said to the black stallion. "I'm gonna go inside and grab a quick slice of pie and a cup of joe."

Izzy entered the diner. Savored the smell of greasy

burgers and greasier potatoes. Fresh java was brewing. A waitress waltzed past carrying a slab of pie buried under a scoop of ice cream the size of a softball. The sweet scents of cinnamon, brown sugar, and pure vanilla swirled up to dance a rumba inside his schnozzle.

Crazy Izzy sighed.

Maybe he'd finally made it to heaven.

He sat at the counter and whistled for a waiter.

"What'll you have?"

"Apple pie all the way. And keep it coming, Mac."

Izzy finished his eleventh slice of apple pie à la mode.

Most of the ice cream had melted into a shallow white lake. So he raised the pie plate to his lips and sucked the sweet, sticky gunk down his gullet.

"You finished?" asked the counterman.

"Bring me another wedge of pie."

"There's none left. You ate it all. You want anything else?"

Norman stood from his stool.

Whipped out his pistol.

Aimed it at a chest-high grease spot on the counterman's apron.

"Grab a little air, pal!"

"What?"

"Put your hands up. I'm skipping out on my tab, see?"

"You won't get far. We've got cameras."

"Cameras? You wanna make me a Hollywood movie star, huh? I'm gonna be in pictures?"

"No. You're gonna be in jail."

"The slammer? In that case, Mac, let's make it worth my while. Pop open the cash box. Fork it over."

The counterman lowered his hands and worked the register keys.

"All of it! That's it. Nice and easy. Put it in a sack and toss in a couple of them cinnamon doughnuts there."

The counterman did as he was told. Norman grabbed the bag and swung around to waggle his rod at the sad saps scurrying for the door or trying to hide under their tables.

"Any of you bunnies get the bright idea to drop a dime and call the coppers, I'll come gunnin' for you, see? Nobody rats out Crazy Izzy Ickleby!" he shouted as he ran out the front door. "Nobody!"

Zack and Judy were driving home to North Chester; Zipper was snoozing in the backseat.

Judy's cell phone rang.

She pulled over to the shoulder of the road so she could answer it.

Zipper woke up so he could eavesdrop. He put his paws on the console between the front seats and leaned in.

"It's your dad," said Judy after glancing at the caller ID window. "Hi, hon. Let me put you on speakerphone. I'm in the car with Zack. What's up?"

"I need to spend the night in the city."

"How come?"

"Big meeting first thing tomorrow. Breakfast with the Pettimore Trust people."

"They're still going to pay for Malik's mom's medical stuff, right?" asked Zack.

"That's why I need to be there. There are a couple board members who want to rescind that offer. I intend to fight for what's right: You guys found the gold, you gave up your share of the reward to Malik and his mom. The board needs to honor that. Malik and his family must be compensated."

"Compensated" was a lawyer word. It meant that his dad would make sure Malik and his family were paid what they'd been promised.

"Since Halloween's over, if everything's more or less settled down at home . . ."

"More or less," said Judy, shrugging at Zack. He gave her a nod of agreement.

More or less. The Icklebys' big night was officially over. They'd all crawled back into their crypt.

"I hate saddling you guys with my aunts. . . ."

"It's more important that you stay there and protect Malik's interests," said Judy. "We'll be fine. The aunts are no trouble."

"Okay. Tell Malik I've got him covered. I'll be home tomorrow night. Love you guys."

"Love you, too. Bye." Judy clicked off the phone.

Zipper cocked his ears. Grumbled.

He heard something.

Now Zack heard it, too: thundering hooves.

"Mom—is there a horse on the highway?"

A giant black stallion came galloping up the road.

It pulled to a stop maybe ten feet in front of where Zack and Judy were parked. The horse snorted loudly, then sniffed the air.

"It must've lost its rider," said Judy.

She climbed out of the car. Zack, too.

"Easy, boy," said Judy. The sleek beast pawed at the pavement and swatted its plumed tail back and forth. Judy reached out for the reins.

The horse reared up on its hind legs and whinnied.

Judy jumped back.

Now the horse let loose a bloodcurdling scream and bolted for the side of the road, where it leapt over the guardrail like it was a hurdle in a show jumping ring.

Clearing the drainage ditch, it tore into the forest and galloped through a thick stand of evergreen trees.

Straight *through* them.

The tree trunks and branches and pine needles passed through its body as if the horse wasn't even there.

"Um, Mom, is that a ghost horse?"

"Yeah," said Judy. "I think so."

"The Haddam Hill Cemetery is on the other side of those trees. Do you think one of those dead Ickleby guys misses his horse?"

"Maybe."

"Okay," said Zack. "Guess we better tell Aunt Ginny she's gonna need one more, jumbo-sized sage candle."

65

Crazy Izzy made Norman's hands jerk the steering wheel hard to the right.

The truck and horse trailer bounded off State Route 13, up the rutted road, and through the wrought-iron cemetery gates. It finally skidded to a stop in front of the Ickleby crypt.

The masked ghost of Barnabas Ickleby stood there waiting.

"Why the rush, Izzy?" asked Barnabas.

"I knocked over a greasy spoon on the way home," said Izzy, climbing out of the truck. "Now the boys in blue are hot on my tail. I figure my getaway vehicle here will be easy for them to spot, on account of the fact there's a horse buggy hitched to its bumper!"

"You found Ebony?"

"Yeah, yeah."

"Let me see Satan's descendant."

"Huh?"

"When I was alive, I rode a black Arabian stallion whom I called Satan."

"Sweet. Hang on." Izzy unlatched the back doors to the horse hauler. The proud horse backed down its metal ramp.

"Excellent," said Barnabas, admiring the animal.

"Okay. Swell. You got your horsey." In the distance, Izzy heard the faint wail of approaching police sirens. "I need to scram."

"Yes, Isador, you do."

Izzy's hands flew up to his head. He felt all kinds of dizzy.

"Hey, what's the big idea?" he moaned. "My noodle feels like it's bein' squeezed in a nutcracker."

"That's me," said Barnabas. "You have served me well. You did your jobs. Now it is time for you to depart that body."

"What? No way. I want to keep on livin'!"

"Sorry. I want to live, too. I just didn't want to bother with *all* the pesky details of organizing my new life."

Izzy was clutching Norman's ears now. He'd never felt a headache like this before. Like sledgehammers to his temples. Sledgehammers and red-hot railroad spikes and tommy guns *rat-a-tat-tat*ting in his brain.

"Depart the body!" Barnabas commanded.

Izzy heard a horse whinny. Then another one. Different-sounding.

Barely able to raise his eyelids, Izzy struggled to look up.

There was another black stallion standing beside Barnabas.

"Enter your offspring!" his masked ancestor shouted. All of a sudden, the ghost horse turned into a blazing ball of purple swamp gas and shot into the live horse's heaving rib cage.

Ebony screamed. Just once. And then he snorted and flicked his mane and scraped at the ground with his hoof as the soul inside tried on its new body for size.

"You chiseled me into helping you bust loose!" Izzy groaned.

"Of course I did," said Barnabas. "I was evil long before you were even born!"

Izzy could feel Norman's body going limp. He slumped to his knees, his arms and neck all rubbery.

"I didn't kill the Jennings kid for ya," he grunted.

"No problem. I will. In fact, I rather enjoy slaying children. And—I was much, much better at it than you."

Now Barnabas was turning into a violet ball of fiery gas.

Izzy felt a sock to his gut.

Everything went purple, then black.

And he was nothing more than a soul without a body again.

The weakened ghost of Crazy Izzy stood beside the truck he had stolen and watched as Norman Ickes, now controlled by Barnabas, marched out of the Ickleby crypt.

The other Icklebys oozed through the walls to watch with him.

Barnabas was carrying a moldy tricornered colonial hat and a sack with some kind of round ball sagging at its bottom. The scrawny little hardware-store clerk looked like he was going to dress up like George Washington and go bowling.

"What's in the bag?" asked Cornelius.

"Insurance."

Barnabas had Norman set the ball bag down on the ground beside the giant black horse. Then he stepped inside the trailer and started rummaging around.

"Now what the heck you lookin' for?" asked Izzy.

Norman came out holding a feed bag, a coil of rope, and a pair of fetlock-trimming scissors.

"These," said Norman, his voice raw and raspy.

"What ho, father?" jibed his son, Lucius. "Do you plan on feeding and grooming your steed?"

"No, you simpering fool."

Izzy watched as the man who looked like Norman cut two pyramid eyes, a nose hole, and a jagged jack-o'-lantern smile into the burlap feed bag.

"I have bridled and saddled my horse. Now I must prepare myself for the journey to come." He glared at Izzy. "Thanks to you, the police are looking for my new face."

Barnabas tugged the burlap bag down over Norman's head and cut a short length of rope to cinch it around the neck. Next he dusted off his worm-eaten tricornered hat—the hat he had been buried in. It fit his newly masked head perfectly.

"You see, dear children," Barnabas croaked, "this is how I fooled everyone into thinking I was a goodly man. I disguised myself whenever I rode the king's highways, pillaging and plundering as the villainous thief known as Jack the Lantern!"

Fully masked, Barnabas worked open the smaller sack and pulled out what Izzy had figured to be a ball.

Only it was a skull.

"Whose head bone is that?" asked Izzy.

"Mine, of course," said Barnabas. "Without it, the three sisters can do nothing more to stop me!"

He jammed the skull into a saddlebag and climbed aboard his muscular steed. Grabbing both reins with one hand, he snicked his tongue. At his slightest tug, the horse moved left, then right, then left again.

Barnabas patted the side of his glistening stallion.

"Good boy, Satan," he whispered.

He raised his right arm. The inky raven fluttered down to perch on it.

The whine of police sirens drew closer. Crazy Izzy felt too queasy to care. Besides, he was a ghost again. The coppers would never even see him hanging around outside the crypt.

"Do you mean to abandon us?" asked Lucius.

"Yes."

"Wait! You cannot do this! You are the head of this family. None of us will know what to do if you are not here to guide us!"

"Too bad!"

Ebony, now Satan, reared up on his hind legs and kicked at the air with his front hooves. The raven took flight. The masked rider raised his cocked hat high above his head.

"Farewell, foolish children! Jack the Lantern rides again!"

Zack and Judy reached the crossroads of Highway 31 and State Route 13.

To the west, they saw the swirling reflection of red police lights.

"You think the ghost horse ran somebody off the road?" asked Zack.

"I guess it's possible. We don't really know all the rules for ghost animals, do we?"

"Not really. There was that crazed cat at the Hanging Hill Playhouse. But it was more like a zombie than a ghost."

They made their way to the Rocky Hill Farms subdivision and cruised up Stonebriar Road to the lip of their driveway.

"Uh-oh," Judy said as glanced up at the house. "More trouble."

"Yeah," said Zack, because he saw it, too: a frantic shadow-puppet show playing on the living room curtains.

A tall woman being chased by three short ones. Several cats flying through the air. Lamps and vases falling willy-nilly.

"Come on," said Judy.

They ran to the house.

The front door flew open.

A tall woman in a business suit stumbled out backward. She was kind of wobbly on her legs, like her high-heel shoes didn't fit.

"I need to see Zachary!"

Uh-oh, Zack thought. The voice sounded familiar.

The tall woman whipped around.

Double uh-oh. It was Aunt Francine.

His dead mother's sister!

"There you are!" said Aunt Francine, her eyes swimming in crazy circles. "Zachary!"

She reached out both arms—Frankenstein-style—and stumbled forward.

"Stand back!" shouted Aunt Ginny as the three Jennings sisters came toddling onto the porch, each one holding a white sage stick. Their three cats streamed out behind them and circled Aunt Francine, who was still staring down at Zack.

Zack took one step backward.

"Where were you?" Aunt Francine demanded.

"We went for a ride," said Judy, stepping in front of Zack to shield him.

"You shouldn't have done that, Judy."

Zack didn't like the way Aunt Francine sounded, because frankly, she sounded just like his dead mother!

"Do I know you?" asked Judy.

Aunt Francine's lips twitched up into the most hideous

smile Zack had ever seen. "We've never been formally introduced, but I know all about you."

"Don't listen to her," cried Aunt Hannah. "That is the dybbuk speaking."

"The what?" said Judy.

"The dybbuk," Aunt Hannah repeated, pronouncing the word "dih-buk."

"That's my aunt Francine," Zack finally blurted. "My real mother's sister."

"That's right, Zachary," said Francine. "Your *real* mother!"

The three sisters circled her on the porch.

"In Jewish folklore," said Aunt Hannah, remaining incredibly calm, "a dybbuk is the malicious disembodied soul of a dead sinner that has attached itself to the body of a living relative."

"Therefore," said Aunt Ginny, "this woman who appears to be Zack's aunt is currently possessed by the soul of someone dead."

"Are you sure about all this?" asked Judy.

"Oh, yes, dearie," said Aunt Ginny. "Quite."

"I had to come back," said the dybbuk. "I did not fulfill my mission in life!"

Aunt Hannah reached into a pouch tied to her belt. "Hear that? Pure dybbuk talk."

"Oh, yes," said Aunt Sophie. "They always say that. Blah-blah-blah 'mission in life.'"

"Leave me alone!" hollered Aunt Francine. "All of

you! I only came back to take care of Zack the way I should have taken care of him when I was alive!"

Zack's jaw fell open.

He knew exactly whose spirit had taken over Aunt Francine's body.

Susan Potter Jennings's.

His dead mother.

Sheriff Ben Hargrove of the North Chester Police Department stood outside the Ickleby crypt on Haddam Hill with a cluster of Connecticut State Police officers.

They were all staring at an empty horse trailer hitched to a pickup truck.

"I can't believe Norman Ickes would do such a thing," said the sheriff, shaking his head.

"Would you like to look at the freeze-frame from the diner's security camera again?" said the state police detective.

"No need," said Hargrove. "I just never pegged Norman to be a violent criminal, waving a gun around like that."

"This the same cemetery where you found the dead girl on Halloween?"

"Yeah," said Hargrove. "You think there's a connection?"

"I'm starting to. This kid, Norman—they sell hunting knives at his hardware store?"

Hargrove nodded. "Herman Ickes, Norman's father, reported one missing last night."

"We'll add it to the list of charges when we nab this guy, which should be soon." The detective gestured toward the empty trailer. "Especially if he's on horseback. Cammie?"

"Yeah, boss?"

"Impound this vehicle and trailer. Haul them over to the crime lab."

"On it."

While the trooper named Cammie radioed for a tow truck, another pair of state police officers came hiking out of the woods.

"Boss?" one of them called out to the lead detective.

"What've you got, MacDonald?"

"This kid Ickes is good."

"How so?"

"We tracked the horse hooves down to a creek."

"Don't tell me: He took the horse into the water?"

"Exactly. We don't know which way he went. Plus, to the south, the creek splits. So . . ."

"Put out an all-points bulletin. I want this Norman's photograph on the eleven o'clock news. I want his description—and the horse's—on the radio. I want every law-abiding citizen in the state of Connecticut looking for Norman Ickes, the Hardware Clerk Crook!"

The three aunts tightened their circle around Aunt Francine.

The cats circling the aunts' ankles hissed, their tiny mouths opening wide to expose needle-sharp fangs.

"Show the dybbuk its false reflection," said Hannah.

The three sisters slowly brought silvery signal mirrors, the kind hikers pack in survival kits, up to their eyes. Zack could see Aunt Francine's face flickering in their flat and shiny surfaces.

She suddenly looked totally paralyzed.

Zack moved closer to Judy.

"She wants to hurt me," he whispered.

"Not to worry, Zack, dear," Aunt Ginny declared from the porch. "This dybbuk shall soon depart."

Aunt Sophie tossed a glittering handful of sparkling powder over Aunt Francine's head.

"Now, if we were ghosts more powerful than the spirit currently possessing the body," explained Aunt Ginny, "we could simply shove the weaker soul out and replace it with one of our own."

"But since we're all alive," said Aunt Sophie, "we must perform an exorcism."

Exorcism? Zack gulped. He had seen that movie on DVD.

"Typically," decreed Aunt Hannah, "this rite is performed by a rabbi and a cohort of ten."

"However," said Aunt Ginny, "we three have streamlined the ceremony to its essence."

"You must have three," said Aunt Hannah.

"Oh, yes," added Aunt Sophie. "Three is the absolute, bare minimum."

Pyewacket, Mister Cookiepants, and Mystic yowled.

"It is time to begin!" said Aunt Hannah.

Aunt Ginny cleared her throat and started to chant: "We three declare it so, the uninvited visitor must now go!"

"Stop!" shrieked the dybbuk. "You stop that this instant!"

Aunt Francine remained frozen in the center of the circle, her arms stubbornly stiff. She couldn't claw but she sure could shriek.

"I want Zack! Stop this foolishness immediately!"

His three great-aunts would not listen to her pleas. They reached out for each other's hands and, swaying slightly side to side, continued their eerie incantation:

"Thrice the brinded cat hath mew'd!"

The black cat in the pack howled loudly.

Zack and Judy stood mesmerized, watching the three women fearlessly circling the snarling demon.

"Round the dybbuk now we go;
Leave this body by the toe.
Spirit, under cold stone lie;
You have had your chance to die."

Aunt Sophie tossed more sparkling powder up into the air.

"Eye of newt and hoof of cow,
Leave this body, leave it now!"

Now Aunt Ginny pulled out a tin party horn, the kind people blow on New Year's Eve.

"In the traditional dybbuk exorcism ritual," she said over her shoulder, "the rabbi would now blow certain strident notes on the shofar, a ram's horn used in Jewish religious ceremonies, to shake loose the soul possessing the body."

"We, however," said Hannah, "have found that any jarring horn will suffice."

"The more sour the notes, the better," added Sophie. "Virginia?"

Aunt Ginny brought the party horn up to her lips and blew a jangled jumble of clashing trumpet honks that sounded like monkey squeals and donkey bleats.

Aunt Francine started to quiver.

And shimmy.

Her body slumped to the floor.

A purple mist seeped up out of her crumpled form.

The violet cloud quickly took shape.

Zack's dead mother, her head bald, her body swallowed up by a hospital gown, her eyes nearly popping out of her skull, stood on the porch, staring down at him.

Zack wasn't sure, but it looked like she might be crying.

71

Her son had grown so much.

"Zachary?" She tried to smile. It wasn't easy. She hadn't done much smiling when she was alive, something she sorely regretted now that she was dead.

"Why did you possess your sister?" asked the woman she recognized as George's aunt Hannah.

"To reach Zack."

"Why?"

"I'm his mother. I know things other spirits cannot!"

"Such as?"

"Grave dangers lie ahead."

"Very well," said Hannah. "Zachary has heard your warning. You may now depart."

Aunt Hannah and her two sisters lit some sort of white torches.

Sage!

Susan Potter froze. She couldn't budge. Could barely speak.

"No . . . the . . . Icklebys," she said, choking.

"Zack knows of the Icklebys," said George's aunt Hannah. "You may now depart."

"Zack?" she pleaded. "I'm . . . different. I . . . made . . . mistakes. Need . . . to . . . make . . . amends!"

Her son hid behind the woman who had taken her place. The stepmother.

"It is time for you to leave here, Susan Potter," George's three aunts chanted. "All is well. There is nothing here for you now."

"Zack . . ."

"All is well. There is nothing here for you now."

"Wait. Zack? Nine-fifty-two."

Thunder cracked. She wasn't allowed to tell him that. It was against the rules.

"Nine-fifty-two!"

Another explosion of heavenly anger. She didn't care.

The stench of the burning sage grew stronger. She could feel herself starting to slip away.

"It is time for you to leave," the aunts chanted again. "All is well. There is nothing here for you now."

"No. Please."

"Go!" she heard Zack shout. "You heard them: There is nothing here for you. Nothing at all! Go and never come back!"

"Zack?" she railed against the coming darkness. "I'm sorry! Nine-fifty-two!"

She had no way of knowing if Zack heard her.

She was alone in the blackness again, doomed to drift once more in the bottomless abyss of her own creation.

Because in death there was no way for Susan Potter Jennings to make right all that in life she had done wrong.

The raven proved an excellent guide, leading horse and rider through the shallows of the Pattakonck River until they came upon a dilapidated boathouse.

Water lapped at the piers of its rotted dock. Barnabas tugged the reins and urged Satan to climb the muddy banks of the river. The hoofprints were the first they had made in miles.

The police searching for Norman Ickes would not be able to track Jack the Lantern.

"Thank you, trusted eyes of the sky," Barnabas said to the bird as it lighted upon his elevated arm. "We need now a stable. Somewhere for Satan to rest this night."

The bird fluttered off its perch and flew up a weed-choked pathway to a dark, deserted mansion. Barnabas snicked his tongue and Satan clip-clopped up the trail of flagstones, following where the bird led.

They soon passed a domed mausoleum penned in by a spike-tipped picket fence. The burial chamber had to be three or four times larger than the Ickleby family crypt.

A name was chiseled above its grand entrance:

SPRATLING

Of course. The dark mansion up ahead was the fabled Spratling Manor, with an estate so vast it had its own monumental burial vault.

Barnabas had heard of this place back when his casket and soul were first wrenched away from the cemetery at Saint Barnabas. A young gravedigger had joked that the Spratlings were "too good" to be buried in Haddam Hill Cemetery with the commoners.

The raven cawed from the peak of a slate roof on an outbuilding.

"A carriage house," murmured Barnabas.

Two wide doors separated by a stone pillar filled the front of the building. Barnabas and his horse trotted closer. Through the narrow glass windows at the top of the roll-up doors, he could see that one stall was occupied by a hulking black Cadillac the size of a boat. The other was empty.

He dismounted his steed.

"You will rest and feed here tonight while I journey north. To Great Barrington."

After removing Satan's bridle and saddle and feeding him a sack of dry oats he found rotting in the mansion's pantry, Barnabas explored the cluttered shelves of the garage.

He found exactly what he was looking for: two kerosene lanterns and a box of wooden matches.

Next he marched back into the manor itself. The place was deserted. Rodents scurrying along the baseboards seemed to be the only living inhabitants.

Passing through a gallery of dark oil portraits, he ascended a staircase to the second floor and started rummaging through closets and storage trunks. The place reeked of mildew and attic dust.

Fortunately, the Spratling men had been old-fashioned when it came to clothing. Barnabas was able to quickly piece together an all-black costume very similar to that worn by his alter ego back in the early 1700s: black riding pantaloons, tasseled Hessian boots, a long black tailcoat, a flowing black cape.

"Forget the cape," said a small voice inside his head.

Barnabas grinned. Norman.

"Why?" he thought back.

"It'll just slow us down."

Us. The thought made Barnabas widen the grin beneath his mask.

"Very well," he said out loud. "I thank you, Norman, for your wise advice and counsel. Now—be still!"

In another closet, Barnabas found a silk top hat. He did not take it.

The black tricorne—stained and weather-beaten, its stiff fabric cracked along the edges—looked much more menacing.

Norman's voice in his head made no objection to his choice of hat.

So Barnabas tugged it on and tucked the pistol his descendant had stolen from the hardware store into his wide leather belt. The modern-day weapon would suffice until Jack the Lantern was reunited with his hidden gold and his own cache of single-shot pistols. He preferred to kill with those. The spark of flint. The roar of the gunpowder. The smoky sizzle of the swirling lead ball ripping through flesh and bone.

It was like shooting a man with a small cannon.

Passing a misty wall mirror, Barnabas gazed upon his gloriously attired reflection. The body of Norman Ickes was slight, but the rippling black garments and sinister jack-o'-lantern mask made him look powerful, especially amidst the gloomy darkness. Pleased with what he saw, Barnabas threw back his head and let loose the lunatic war cry of a madman.

Jack the Lantern was back.

73

Randy Lawson was driving home on State Route 13.

It had been a long day. Sales calls in Waterbury and Danbury. Dinner with a client. Now he was traveling the empty backcountry roads through Connecticut to Massachusetts.

He had just passed the imposing iron gates leading into somebody's grand estate when a massive fireball, like a tanker truck exploding, erupted in the middle of the highway.

He stomped on the brakes.

His car came to a tire-screeching stop ten feet in front of the roiling inferno as it belched out thick clouds of curling black smoke. Someone had tossed two kerosene lanterns onto the asphalt!

Fortunately, Randy Lawson wasn't hurt. The seat belt had done its job. The air bags had not deployed.

But now his heart started racing even faster.

A masked man, dressed all in black, who looked like a

walking jack-o'-lantern in a three-cornered hat, came striding out of the thicket at the side of the road.

He carried a pistol.

"Take me to Saint Barnabas church in Great Barrington," croaked the masked man. "Or die!"

All of Zack's aunts—the great and, Francine, the not-so-great—were gathered in the kitchen.

Judy turned on the small TV in the breakfast nook to check out the eleven o'clock local news. "I wonder if they'll have anything about whatever was going on up at the graveyard."

Aunt Ginny arched an eyebrow. "The Haddam Hill Cemetery?"

"Yeah," said Zack. "We saw a bunch of swirling police lights up that way when we were driving home."

"Sisters?" said Aunt Hannah, sounding mad. "Family meeting. Outside. Now! And this time, Virginia, you *will* tell us the truth!"

Hannah, Sophie, Ginny, and their cats scampered out the back door to the deck.

"Excuse me," said Aunt Francine, her voice groggy. "Might I trouble you people for a glass of water?"

"Of course," said Judy. "Zack?"

"Got it." He grabbed a glass from the cupboard and filled it with tap water.

"Don't you have bottled water?"

"Sorry," said Zack.

"Never mind, then." She fumbled in her jacket for a pack of cigarettes.

"Um, there's no smoking allowed in this house," said Judy.

"Don't be ridiculous. I've had a very difficult night."

"Sorry."

Aunt Francine fumed. It was very similar to the way Zack's real mother used to fume. Zack figured fuming ran in the family.

"Who, exactly, are you again?" Aunt Francine said to Judy.

"She's my mom," said Zack.

"Was I talking to you, Zachary?"

Zack looked down at his shoes. "No."

"I didn't think so. So tell me, Judy, did George hide his son's existence while you two were dating? Is that how he tricked you into becoming his stepmother?"

"Ms. Potter," said Judy, "I love my son."

"Really? Where is he? I'd love to meet him."

Zack had heard enough. He looked Aunt Francine straight in the eyes. "How come you have to act this way?"

"What?"

"All mean and bitter and nasty."

"How dare you speak to me like that! Children should be seen, not heard."

"Says who?" asked Judy.

"Well, that's certainly how my parents raised Susan and me. I see you and George have decided to take a more liberal approach."

"I think you should leave," said Judy. "Now."

"What?"

"There's a motel two miles up the highway. You shouldn't drive back to Boston tonight, not in your condition. I'll book you a room with our credit card."

Aunt Francine stood up, fumbled again for her cigarettes. "I don't even know why I came here. One minute I'm home dealing with beggars at my doorstep; the next I'm here with the smart-mouthed brat who killed my sister."

Judy narrowed her eyes. "I'll call the motel."

"My, aren't you congenial?" And with that, Aunt Francine stormed out of the house, furiously flicking her cigarette lighter the whole way.

"What a monster," muttered Judy.

"Yeah," said Zack with a smile. "But you know what, Mom?"

"What?"

"When it comes to slaying monsters, you and me make a pretty good team."

The three great-aunts paraded back into the kitchen.

"Judy? Zack?" said Aunt Hannah. "We need to go up to the Haddam Hill Cemetery and deal with the Icklebys."

"Like you guys did back in 1979?" said Zack.

Aunt Ginny looked surprised. "What do you know about 1979?"

"Zack and I talked to Father Abercrombie today," said Judy.

"Really?" sniffed Hannah.

"He told us that you three were the ones who arranged to have the Ickleby caskets moved to North Chester."

"We had to," said Sophie. "Those twelve ghosts were making so much mischief up in Massachusetts. Why, they even killed a cat. Grizzmaldo." She made a slicing gesture across her throat.

Pyewacket, Mister Cookiepants, and Mystic meowed in disgust.

"So are you guys gonna go fumigate the whole crypt with sage candles?" asked Zack.

"No," said Aunt Hannah with a scowl at Aunt Ginny. "We're going to lock them back up. Zack, we need the sealing charm."

Now Zack was confused. "Huh?"

"When we put the Ickleby coffins into the abandoned Spratling crypt, we fashioned a special lock to prevent their spirits from ever escaping their new resting place."

"Even on Halloween," added Aunt Sophie.

"Now, it seems," said Aunt Hannah, "someone has broken open that seal."

Aunt Ginny turned to Zack. "I'm sorry, dear, but it's true: Pyewacket and I conspired to have you and your friends pry open the sealing stone."

"Really?" said Zack. "'Cause I don't think we did."

Ginny smiled. "Oh, you did. That's why the Ickleby spirits are on the prowl. I had hoped we might be able to take them out, one by one—like we did with Eddie Boy and Little Paulie."

"We don't blame you or your friends," said Hannah.

"But we need to lock 'em back up, Zack," said Sophie. "Before they cause any more trouble."

"Like whatever happened at the cemetery tonight," added Hannah. "All those police cars you saw."

"Zack," said Ginny, "we need the charm back."

"But I didn't take it."

Now all three Jennings sisters were staring at him.

The way Zack's mother used to stare at him when she swore he was lying.

Zack held up his right hand like he was taking an oath.

"I promise. I did not take a 'sealing charm.'"

"Did you happen upon a black stone shaped like a heart?" asked Aunt Ginny.

"Oh, you mean the 3-D puzzle?"

"You could call it that."

"It had all sorts of interlocking pieces and a smaller, even blacker heart hidden in the middle?" Zack said.

"That's right. And what did you do with this black heart stone, Zack?"

"Malik, who's really good with puzzles and junk, he took it apart."

The three sisters nodded. The cats meowed.

"And thus the spell was broken," said Hannah. "Zachary, we need it back."

Zack remembered what Mad Dog Murphy had said in the corn maze: *Little Paulie's a pal of mine. Now Paulie wants out. So give his people what they're looking for.*

The black heart stone!

"Um, I don't have it."

"Oh, dear," said Aunt Ginny. "Who does?"

"Oh my goodness," said Judy.

Something on the TV news had caught her eye: security camera footage of a man robbing a diner.

And not just any man.

Norman Ickes. Malik's friend at the hardware store.

"Turn it up," said Zack. "Hurry!"

Judy pressed the volume button.

"Police are searching for North Chester resident Norman Ickes in connection with the robbery of the Hi-Way 31 Eat and Run, even though, while committing the crime, Ickes attempted to throw police off his track by using an alias."

The shot moved in tighter on the footage and captioned what Norman was saying:

"Nobody rats out Crazy Izzy Ickleby. Nobody!"

"Ickleby?" said Judy.

"Oh, dear," said Ginny, holding on to the counter so she wouldn't faint. "This is worse than we could have imagined. They found a body. A blood relation."

"That's right!" said Judy. "Father Abercrombie told us Norman Ickes was actually an Ickleby!"

"Oh, my," gasped Sophie. "They've gone dybbuk on us, too!"

"Zack," said Ginny, "we need to retrieve the black heart stone. We need to do so immediately."

"Who has it, Zack?" asked Judy. "Malik?"

Zack shook his head and pointed to the face on TV. "No. His friend. Norman Ickes."

"This is the place," rasped Jack the Lantern as the car he had hijacked pulled into what was left of the asphalt driveway leading down to Saint Barnabas church.

A man holding out a trembling flashlight came out of the ramshackle rectory house. Flickering shadows danced across his anguished face.

"Who's there? Who are you?"

Even from fifty feet away, the soul inside Norman Ickes's body recognized the nervous old man.

"Father Clayton Abercrombie," he whispered with great satisfaction.

He turned to his driver.

"Mr. Lawson?"

"Y-y-yes?"

"Thank you very kindly for the ride."

"Bop him on the head!" urged Norman's voice inside Jack's head. *"Use the gun Izzy stole!"*

"What an excellent suggestion," said the masked highwayman.

"What?" said the driver. "I didn't suggest any—"

Jack the Lantern knocked the man out cold with the butt of his pistol.

"*Ooh,*" purred Norman's voice. "*I love doing that.*"

"What's going on up there?" Jack the Lantern heard Father Abercrombie cry.

Taking strides as long as Norman's legs would allow, he swept down the hill toward the churchyard, where Father Abercrombie stood quaking like a branch full of dead leaves.

The church building behind the priest was not at all as Jack remembered it. The stained glass windows lacked life or color, for there were no lights burning inside the house of God. *How fitting,* he thought. *God has lost. The darkness has won.*

"Good evening, Father Abercrombie."

"Who are you?"

"An old friend of this humble chapel."

"Why do you wear that mask?"

"So you might know who I truly am."

Father Abercrombie's lips quivered. "Wh-wh-who, then, are you?"

"In my time, many called me Jack the Lantern. Though here, in this place, I was known as Saint Barnabas's most generous benefactor."

"What?"

"Allow me to introduce myself, Father Abercrombie." He dipped into a grand bow. "I, sir, am Squire Barnabas Ickleby, the man for whom this church was named!"

70

Zack, Judy, and the three aunts were glued to the television set.

A photograph of Norman Ickes filled the screen. "According to Connecticut State Police, Ickes also stole a thoroughbred racehorse from Stansbury Stables earlier this afternoon. . . ."

"Sisters?" said Aunt Ginny, regaining her old spunk. "Since the black heart stone is now in the hands of the enemy, we have no choice but to forge a new one."

"But how?" Sophie said, fretting. "Can we still extract the key ingredient?"

"Certainly," said Ginny. "The first Ickleby to ever set foot in America is still entombed on Haddam Hill; his coffin is still clearly marked with the Ickleby family crest and a rather large 'B,' as I recall."

"Virginia is correct," said Hannah. "We must forge a new stone and reimprison the spirits."

"Even though—as I said earlier—I fear it is but a temporary solution," said Ginny.

"Temporary? What do you mean?" asked Judy.

"Oh, don't worry, dear," said Ginny, pretending to be perky. "A temporary solution is better than no solution at all. Pack your gear, girls. We're going back to Haddam Hill."

Aunts Hannah and Sophie bustled out of the kitchen. Ginny turned to Zack and Judy.

"Do you have a pair of pliers?"

"Sure," said Zack. "But why do you need pliers?"

"To remove something from inside the Ickleby crypt."

"Open it," snarled Jack the Lantern as Father Abercrombie fumbled through his heavy key ring, searching for the skeleton key to the hardened steel lock on the empty Ickleby crypt.

"M-maybe," the priest stammered, "you might find what you seek inside the church?"

"No. The crypt is where I hid my two strongboxes many, many years ago."

"Two?" said Father Abercrombie, sounding surprised.

Jack put a hand on Father Abercrombie's shoulder. The squirmy old man looked up, fear filling his eyes.

"Tell me, Padre, did you or your predecessors happen to chance upon my buried treasures?"

Father Abercrombie swallowed hard. "Just the one."

"I see," croaked Jack, icy calm in his voice. "Which one? The guns or the gold?"

"I didn't mean to. I swear by all that is sacred. I was simply—"

"Which one? The guns or the gold?"

Another hard swallow.

"The gold."

"I see. And how much did you leave for me?"

"This was fifteen, twenty years ago. After my wife died. After my congregation dwindled and there wasn't enough money in the collection plate to—"

Jack grabbed Father Abercrombie by the collar and raised him off the ground. The longer he remained inside Norman Ickes's body, the stronger the young man became, his muscles fueled by Barnabas Ickleby's surging hatred and rage.

"How much is left, old man?"

"None! I spent it all!"

Jack opened his hand and let the priest fall.

"Very well," he said, the calm returning to his croaking voice. "'Tis but a minor setback. For as long as there are children to kidnap and hold for ransom, Jack the Lantern can always acquire more gold. However, to do so, I will most assuredly need my old weapons."

"Your weapons?"

"Yes. Unlock the lock, you sniveling worm!"

The priest did as he was told.

80

Zipper led the way up Haddam Hill to the cemetery.

Zack, Judy, and Aunt Ginny were right behind him; the other two aunts were right behind them.

Aunt Ginny was carrying her stuffed carpetbag, which looked like something Mary Poppins would bring on a nanny job. Zack figured it was full of sage candles, potions, and powders—plus all the pliers he had grabbed from his dad's toolbox out in the garage.

"Aunt Ginny?" said Zack.

"Yes, dear?"

"Can I ask you a question?"

"Of course."

"Back in 1979, why didn't you guys just toss a bunch of sage grenades into that first Ickleby crypt, the one at Saint Barnabas church, and get rid of all the evil spirits?"

"Sage only stuns ghosts who have fully materialized."

"So you have to see 'em to freeze 'em?"

"Well put, Zack. That's exactly why we need to make

a new sealing stone—to lock up all the evil Ickleby souls who have not yet found a blood relative to dybbuk. As for Crazy Izzy—well, I suppose we'll need to do an exorcism on Norman Ickes the minute the police arrest him."

"How long will it take to make a new black heart stone?" asked Judy.

"Several days, I'm afraid. Creating the outer shell is actually the easy part. We simply need to acquire the services of a sculptor who knows how to work with obsidian. The blacker heart at the center, that's a bit more complicated."

"Because it's so tiny?" said Zack.

"It's not the size that makes the process difficult. What's hard is capturing and distilling the essence of a family's soul."

"Wow," said Judy. "How do you do that?"

"Well, first we must obtain a tooth from the eldest ancestor available to us—in this case, Barnabas."

"A tooth?" Zack and Judy said at the same time.

"That's right. Teeth last a very long time after death and retain the traits passed on from generation to generation."

"You mean a family's genes and DNA?" said Judy.

"That and all the good and bad carried across generations. The kind words spoken as well as the evil thoughts bit back. The holy prayers uttered and the foul curses sworn. Any tooth decay will, of course, hint at an evil festering beneath a deceptively bright and shiny surface. Oh, yes, when you extract a tooth from a dead man's skull, you glean much, much more than a molar or a bicuspid. You see, teeth, just like families, have deep roots. Extract a tooth and you will extract a family's true identity."

"Oh-kay," said Judy. "If you say so."

"Um," said Zack, "have you told any dentists about this?"

"No, dear. It might give them delusions of grandeur. Now, once you have the tooth, you must smelt it with certain acids and mix it with onyx crystals while you chant a few very powerful words only . . . herbologists . . . know. And, you must be very, very careful while handling the finished onyx heart."

"How come?"

"If that heart shatters, the soul of the man whose tooth you used to create it will be sent straight to the underworld."

"Barnabas, right?"

Aunt Ginny nodded.

"But he was a good guy."

"Exactly. That's why we must be careful. We don't want to accidentally send a good soul like Barnabas . . . *downstairs*. We simply used his tooth because he was the oldest Ickleby we could locate in America."

Zack's foot slipped in a muddy furrow.

"Wow. Check out all these tire tracks," he said, looking down and studying the graveyard's rutted dirt road.

"This is where the police cars were, I'll bet," said Judy.

"Maybe this is the only hideout Crazy Izzy knew," said Zack. "Maybe he brought Norman's body up here to hide."

"I don't know, Zack," said Judy. "There were a lot of police. They would've found him. Right?"

She sounded unsure.

Zack could relate.

What if Crazy Izzy, who, after all, had been a gangster, had outfoxed Sheriff Hargrove? What if he'd crawled into a crypt, opened a casket, shoved aside a skeleton, and lowered the lid or something?

Judy swung her flashlight from side to side; its beam cut across headstones and marble crosses and weeping angel statues.

No Norman, thank goodness.

Zack looked at the Ickleby crypt.

The heart-shaped lock had been busted open. It was dangling from its hasp between the two wooden doors.

He heard a squishy noise behind him.

"Oh, dear," said Aunt Ginny, bracing her hand against a gravestone so she could examine her shoe. "I believe I just stepped in horse poop."

Zipper trotted over to sniff the sole. Zack could see a big glob of straw-flecked muck at the base of Aunt Ginny's heel. Horse poop.

"Aunt Ginny?" said Zack.

"Yes, dear?"

"When we accidentally opened the black heart stone,

would that automatically make the lock on the Ickleby crypt pop open, too?"

"No, dear. The black heart stone functions on a different metaphysical plane than an actual lock."

"Then somebody broke open the real one, because it was clamped shut the last time I was up here."

Judy gasped. "Horse poop!"

"I beg your pardon?" said Aunt Hannah.

"The TV said Norman stole a horse."

"Oh, my," said Aunt Sophie.

"Zack's right," said Judy. "The dybbuk could still be here. We need to call the police."

Just then, a ghost materialized—at the entrance to the Ickleby crypt!

81

Zack was standing closest to the ghost.

This one was wearing a three-piece striped suit, a necktie with hula girls painted on it, and an old-fashioned fedora. He looked like the mobsters in black-and-white movies. He also looked like he'd just lost a boxing match or something.

"Go ahead, you dirty rats," the ghost groaned, doubled over with pain. "Call the coppers. See if I care! That grifter turned me into a stinking patsy."

"Um, are you Crazy Izzy Ickleby?" Zack asked, remembering the name from the TV news.

"Yeah, kid. That's my name. Don't wear it out."

"Crazy Izzy!" shouted Aunt Sophie. "That's our Ickleby! The one we're looking for!" She sparked the tip of a sage flare and tossed it at Crazy Izzy's feet. "Hurry, girls! We've got him!"

"Wait," coughed Izzy, who, thanks to the sage, couldn't budge. "Cut me some slack, toots. . . ."

Aunt Sophie started chanting.

"It is time for you to leave here."

Hannah and Ginny joined in.

"All is well. There is nothing here for you now."

Crazy Izzy was starting to fade. "You ditzy dames. Why you doin' this to me? I ain't done nothin' to youse!"

The three sisters chanted faster.

"Itistimeforyoutoleavehere. Alliswell. Thereisnothing-hereforyounow."

"I ain't the one you want!"

Crazy Izzy vanished.

"Quick," said Aunt Ginny. "Look for Norman Ickes. The dybbuk was foolish enough to exit his body. Hope-fully, the real Norman is somewhere close by and is still in possession of the original black heart stone!"

"Mr. Ickes is most likely exhausted by his unwelcomed possession," said Aunt Hannah. "He could be sleeping it off."

"The crypt!" said Aunt Sophie. "He's probably inside the crypt, taking a nap!"

"Hurry," said Aunt Ginny. "If he still has the charm, we can lock them all away again!"

Zipper barked.

Zack bolted for the mausoleum doors.

Before he could grab the handles, another ghost materialized—right on the front step!

Zack yanked back his hand. His arm prickled with icy goose bumps as it passed through the specter's materializ-ing form.

This Ickleby ghost looked like a riverboat gambler.

"My goodness, Zachary, back again? You certainly are a bothersome brat, much like a booger we simply can't thump off."

"Where's Norman Ickes?" said Zack.

"The hardware-store clerk?"

"Yeah. We need to talk to him."

"Oh, Norman's not talking to anyone tonight."

"Why not?"

"Barnabas won't let him."

02

Barnabas Ickleby, disguised as Jack the Lantern, used
Norman Ickes's body to mark off ten paces from the door
of the original Ickleby crypt to the center of the empty
tomb.

". . . eight, nine, ten."

When he reached that spot, he turned to the south and
marked off ten more. He turned once more and marched
off five long strides.

Then he stopped and gazed down at the scuffed soil
near the pointy tips of his riding boots.

"Is that where you hid your weapons?" asked Father
Abercrombie, cowering under a cramped stone archway.

"Yes!" croaked Jack. "Before I died, I built this crypt
and secretly hid my treasures! The gold, which you, good
father, stole from me, and a fine arsenal of hand-tooled
weapons!"

Jack dropped to his knees to claw at the dirt with
his fingers.

"Guns will provide the quickest means for me to replenish the treasure you purloined. And what's the sense of being alive if I am not rich, as well?"

Raking his hands across the hard-packed soil, he gouged out first a shallow hole and then a deeper trench.

"Huzzah!" he shouted when he uncovered his first glimpse of the strongbox's rusty steel lid. "I am once more complete!"

63

"So where exactly is Norman Ickes?" Zack asked the ghost of the riverboat gambler. "We need to find him."

"He went for a horseback ride." The gambler looked past Zack and sneered at the three great-aunts. "Good evening, ladies."

"Where's Norman?" Zack asked again, louder this time.

"Silly boy. Barnabas and the hardware-store clerk are long gone."

"Wait a minute," said Judy. "Crazy Izzy was the one inside Norman at the diner."

"Yes, but that was before Barnabas decided it was *his* turn to pillage and plunder."

Another Ickleby faded into view. This one was wearing a powdered wig and looked like the guys who signed the Declaration of Independence. "You simpering fools. Barnabas, my villainous grandfather, has absconded with the body you seek."

"Barnabas was evil, too?" said Zack.

"Ha! He was the most evil of us all!"

Three more Icklebys, all from the 1800s, judging by their clothes and goofy sideburns, appeared outside the crypt.

"He longed to ride again!" said one.

"To terrorize the king's highway as Jack the Lantern," said another.

"Who's Jack the Lantern?" asked Judy.

"The infamous child snatcher," said the man in the Paul Revere wig. "The blackest sheep of our entire family! The one who showed us all the way, who set us on the path to perdition!"

"Why, if it weren't for Barnabas," said the riverboat gambler, "we all would have lived very boring lives."

"Deaths, too!" added one of the guys with mutton-chop sideburns, which connected under his nose.

Now all nine of the lingering Ickleby souls were laughing outside the mausoleum bearing their name.

"Barnabas done took off," wheezed a toothless gold miner in a beat-up ten-gallon hat. "And y'all ain't never gonna catch him, neither! Come on, fellers, let's vamoose before these three set in to tossin' Injun sage sticks at us."

All of a sudden, the nine gloating ghosts looked lost. Like kids in the mall who can't find their parents.

"Capital idea," said the one in the powdered wig. "But where shall we flee?"

"How the heck should I know?" said the gold miner. "I ain't no Barnabas."

"Well, we need to flee—somewhere."

And then they started bickering.

"Well, if I knew where in tarnation to flee, I would have already fled there!"

"Barnabas deserted us."

"We must fend for ourselves!"

"A most excellent suggestion. Tell me how, and I shall!"

"Wait," said Zack. "The black heart stone! Where is it?"

"Why, we haven't a clue," sneered a vain dandy with golden ringlets. "None of us has ever ventured beyond this cemetery."

"Then who hid the stone?" demanded Zack.

"Why, Crazy Izzy, of course. I'm sure he'd be happy to tell you exactly where Barnabas told him to stash the stone, but, alas, he no longer can."

"'Cause you dang fools done chanted him off to kingdom come!" wheezed the miner, slapping his dusty knee. "You ain't never gonna find that dang stone!"

All nine ghosts—none of whom, it seemed to Zack, could think, scheme, or plan without Barnabas's help—were weeping with laughter when they really should've been busy escaping.

However, all nine stopped chuckling the instant they heard a cat howl so loudly it made Zipper jump behind a gravestone to hide.

The first ghost cat Zack saw materialize was black and rippled with muscles—just like the Black Shuck dog.

It was also headless.

"Grizzmaldo!" gasped Aunt Ginny. "That's our cousin Harriet's kitty!"

Fiendishly angry at the Icklebys for what they had done to him on that long-ago Halloween night, Grizzmaldo swiped at the nine terrified ghosts with claws as long and as sharp as steak knives. He shrieked at the trembling demons through the gaping hole that used to be his throat.

Now the cemetery was swarming with hissing ghost cats. A dozen. Then two dozen. Then a hundred. Maybe two hundred. And all of them looked like they had been abused in life. Some had charred tail fur. Others limped. Several were missing eyes or ears or limbs.

The swarm of cats let loose a chorus of bawling caterwauling so deafening, Zack thought he was at a day care center where they had forgotten to feed all the babies.

And he remembered the cat cries he had heard when he and Zip chased the Black Shuck dog up Haddam Hill.

Zack figured that the headless cat, Grizzmaldo, had been biding his time—watching the Ickleby crypt, waiting for his chance to wreak revenge by mustering up his own phantom army of mistreated mousers.

As the undulating ocean of ruffled fur, mangled tails, and flared fangs prowled closer, the nine Ickleby fiends stood cowering at the door to their crypt.

"Sisters?" whispered Aunt Ginny. "Sage candles! Quickly, now!"

All three sisters lit smudge sticks and hurled them up over the writhing wall of ghost cats.

Three volleys of three flares.

Nine all together.

One for each immortal soul.

When the Ickleby ghosts froze, the sisters started to chant.

"There is nothing here for you now. . . ."

father Abercrombie watched as Jack the Lantern hoisted the corroded strongbox out of the ground and pried the chest open.

"There you are, my pretties," he said, removing the first of several cloth-wrapped bundles. Unfurling the sheathing, he revealed a gleaming pistol with a shiny brass barrel, ornate scrolling on the trigger, and a stock made of burnished wood.

"A fine-quality English flintlock pistol, handcrafted for me in 1740," the monster sighed. He quickly unwrapped another pistol, a powder cask, and a leather bag full of bullets that clacked against each other like lead marbles.

He tucked the two pistols into his wide leather belt.

He reached into the open metal trunk one more time

and pulled out the last weapon: a sinister-looking sword with rust stains splotching the blade.

As if he could read the priest's mind, the demon in the tricornered hat looked up, the devil's own grin slashed across his mask.

"That isn't rust, Padre. It's blood."

86

The nine ghosts were gone before the aunts finished chanting "there is nothing here for you" the second time.

Aunt Sophie pulled out a tiny spiral notebook and a stubby miniature-golf pencil. "Let's see. These nine, plus Crazy Izzy, Little Paulie, and Eddie Boy. Nine plus one, carry the one, plus one, plus . . ."

"That is all twelve, Sophia," said Aunt Hannah.

"Leaving us Barnabas," said Aunt Ginny. "Who, they now inform us, was the worst Ickleby of all."

Aunt Hannah nodded. "We must imprison the great deceiver's soul."

"We will," said Aunt Ginny. "Just as soon as we forge a new sealing stone." She unclasped her carpetbag and rummaged around inside. "Ah! Just what the doctor ordered." She pulled out a pair of long-handled pliers. "Or, in this case, the dentist."

"What are you going to do?" asked Zack.

"March into that crypt and yank out another tooth from that old phony's skull!"

07

Jack the Lantern marched Father Abercrombie out of the empty Ickleby crypt, past the church.

"You will now drive me south to Spratling Manor," he said, poking the priest in the ribs with both pistols.

"Spratling Manor? In North Chester?"

"Yes! The town where you shipped our boxed-up bones all those years ago. I must go there to slay the youngest member of the Jennings clan."

"The sheriff's grandson? Why?"

"To avenge my family's honor. Once the lad is dead, I will rebuild my fortune."

"How?"

"Stealing children. Holding them for ransom or selling them into slavery. I have always found child snatching to be a swift path to riches."

They reached the car. Its owner, Mr. Lawson, was still conked out behind the wheel.

"Oh, my," gasped the priest.

Jack yanked the unconscious driver out of the car.

"Just leave him in the ditch!" the voice of Norman suggested in Jack's head.

"I should slay him," Jack thought back.

"Don't waste your ammunition on a pawn! Save your bullets for snatching children and killing Snertz."

"But . . ."

"If you kill him, more police will be on your tail. They will hunt you down and slap you in irons before you reap your riches."

"The move you suggest seems wise."

"Of course it is! I was captain of the chess team! Leave him here and flee the scene!"

Jack cocked back the hammers on both pistols. Aimed them at Father Abercrombie.

"Drive me south to North Chester. Make haste."

"Of course." The nervous priest climbed into the horseless carriage.

"Tell the coward to drive slowly!" the voice of Norman instructed his dybbuk. *"We don't want the police pulling you over for speeding."*

"Drive slowly," Jack said to the priest. "We are in no rush. I'm certain the good boys and girls of North Chester are all abed at this hour. I shan't be able to snatch them until tomorrow morning."

"You mean when they're on their way to school?"

Jack smiled beneath his grinning mask.

"Why, Padre, what an excellent suggestion!"

88

Zack, Judy, Zipper, and Aunt Ginny crept into the Ickleby family crypt on Haddam Hill with their flashlights.

Aunts Sophie and Hannah would "wait outside, thank you very much."

Zack had never been inside a tomb before.

The flaking plaster walls were caked with black stains, covered with mold and mildew. They were so crackled you could see the exterior blocks and the lumpy mortar slathered between.

Zack swung his flashlight over to a stack of three coffins. One was dark brown wood; one seemed to be gilded with gold. The third was a rotting pine box with its knotholes popped out. Zack heard a tiny squeak and almost dropped his light when he saw a mouse scurry out of the coffin.

"Where's Barnabas?" asked Judy.

"I'm not sure," said Aunt Ginny. "The coffins have shifted positions since the workmen placed them here all those years ago."

Great, thought Zack. *The ghosts have spent thirty-some years in here playing musical coffins.*

"As I recall, the oldest coffin looks like a mummy's casket made out of iron," said Aunt Ginny. "The Ickleby family crest and the letter 'B' are emblazoned on its top."

Zack and Zipper drifted off to explore one corner of the crypt while Judy and Aunt Ginny moved to the opposite end of the dank tomb.

Zipper barked. Zack raised the beam of his light and saw a long box made out of gray washtub metal. There were handles on the side, a hump in the middle for the chest, and a bigger bump at the bottom for feet. The lid over where the head would be was already open.

Zack moved forward, saw the family crest and big letter "B" on the coffin cover.

He looked down into the head hole.

He wished he hadn't.

"You guys? I think somebody got here before us."

Judy and Aunt Ginny hurried over.

"Oh, my," said Aunt Ginny. "That's inconvenient."

"Yeah," said Zack.

Inside the coffin was a skeleton.

Well, the collarbone and rib cage.

No head, though.

Someone had stolen the skull.

Which meant they had taken all the teeth, too.

"That settles it," said Aunt Ginny with a defeated sigh. "We must find the original black heart stone. It's our only hope!"

"So, this is Spratling Manor?" said the nervous priest as he drove the stolen car under the arched gates at the entrance to the estate.

"Yes," croaked his masked passenger.

"They're the ones who had the spare burial chamber," Father Abercrombie prattled on. "The Spratlings. Unusual name. One you remember. Spratling."

"Pull up to the carriage house."

A black raven cawed at them from its perch on the building's roof.

"A crow sitting on a house is an evil omen," commented the priest. "It means someone will die here. Tonight."

The masked man gestured with his twin pistols. "Step out."

"It's late. I really should head back to—"

"Out! Now!"

The priest stepped out of the car. The raven swooped down to land with a hollow thud on top of the automobile.

Jack the Lantern extended his arm. The bird hopped over to it like a falcon to a falconer.

"Fly, my dark friend. Seek out the Jennings boy. Bring me word of his whereabouts, for come the new day, I shall head out to strike him down."

The bird took off like a shot, its broad black wings blocking out the moon as it circled overhead.

Much to Father Abercrombie's surprise, the masked man brought a hand up to his jagged mouth hole and yawned.

"I must rest. I have become uncomfortably drowsy. I had forgotten how human bodies wear down on a daily basis."

"Yes," said Father Abercrombie urgently. "Sleep will do you good. It's so quiet and peaceful here, you should sleep quite soundly. No noise at all . . ."

"There is no noise because we are surrounded by forest, Father. The trees swallow up all sound." Jack the Lantern once more raised his double pistols. "By the by, that evil omen you spoke of will prove true. Someone will, indeed, die at this house tonight. You."

The devil squeezed the triggers. Two flints sparked.

Father Abercrombie heard the roar of the twin gunpowder blasts.

And then he heard nothing.

"Try to get some rest, you guys," Judy said to Zack and Zipper as she switched off the lights in the basement rumpus room. "I have a feeling tomorrow's going to be a busy day."

"So no school?" asked Zack from the sofa bed.

"No. Your dad and I just discussed it on the phone. Too many Icklebys had 'hurt Zack Jennings' on their To Do List. Barnabas probably does, too."

Zack nodded. "Payback for Dad's aunts yanking out his tooth."

"Exactly. So you and Zip are with me until the police arrest Norman Ickes."

Zack was exhausted and quickly fell asleep.

He had a horrible dream about mice playing card games in coffins with crazed cats, followed by another, featuring headless skeletons being chased by a demented dentist screaming, "Did you floss between your ribs?"

Around three in the morning, Zack woke up when he once again heard heavy panting and the sloppy sound of dribbling dog drool.

He peeled open an eye and looked over at the battered lounge chair. His grandfather was sitting there, petting the slobbering Black Shuck dog, who had dimmed his eyeballs to an orangish night-light glow.

"Hey, Grandpa."

"Zack. How you holding up, champ?"

"Pretty good, I guess. Your sisters sent a dozen Ickleby souls on to, well, wherever it is souls like that go. But now we have to find the black heart stone we gave to Norman so we can seal up Barnabas, who everybody thought was a good guy, but, it turns out, he's where the evil all started."

Grandpa Jim nodded.

"But," said Zack, "there's only one problem: Nobody knows where the black heart stone is except Norman or Barnabas or maybe this ghost named Crazy Izzy Ickleby, but your sisters already sent him away and . . ."

Zack saw a strange look flicker across his grandfather's sparkling blue eyes.

"What?" he said. "Do you know where Crazy Izzy hid the stone?"

Now Grandpa Jim squirmed in his chair.

"Even if I do, Zack, I can't come right out and tell you."

"Are those guys upstairs ever going to change these

stupid rules? Because I gotta tell you, Grandpa, they sure make dealing with demons a whole lot harder than it has to be."

"And when I tell you about the stone, should I tell you who thinks you're the cutest boy in the whole sixth grade?"

"Well, you don't have to tell me *everything*. You can definitely skip the mushy junk."

"I'm trying to make a point here, Zack."

"I know. Oh, did you hear? My real mother popped by for a visit."

"I know." Grandpa Jim leaned forward and looked around to make sure nobody was listening (even though nobody else was in the basement, just the two dogs). "You should listen to what your mother told you tonight."

"Really?"

"She isn't like she used to be, champ. Dying changes a person. Makes them regret the mistakes they made when they were alive."

"Have you seen her?"

"No. But, well, I've heard things. Susan Potter is working hard, trying to . . ."

Zack heard the distant rumble of thunder.

Grandpa Jim shook his head. "I swear, they have ears everywhere."

"What? Who?"

"Nothin'. I said too much." Grandpa Jim started to fade into his chair, the dog into the carpet. "Listen to what your mother told you, Zack. Right before she vanished. Listen good!"

The Black Shuck dog disappeared.

Grandpa Jim lingered for a moment longer, worry lines creasing his face.

Then he vanished, too.

91

No way could Zack go right back to sleep.

So he climbed up the stairs and headed for the kitchen.

Zipper padded after him.

They could both use a snack, maybe some milk that wasn't chocolate, which was all they had in the basement fridge.

You should listen to what your mother told you.

Okay. That was a clue of some kind. The only hint Grandpa Jim could give (on account of the rules) without being sent to the big detention hall in the sky.

Zack gave Zipper a dog biscuit. Poured himself a glass of milk. When he sat down at the table to drink it and stare out the windows, Zipper hopped up into his lap, leaving the bone-shaped biscuit on the floor.

Zack figured his dog had seen enough bones for one night. He stroked the fur behind Zip's ears and thought.

What had his mother said?

I'm different. I made mistakes.

Then she sort of sounded like she was begging for forgiveness.

Need . . . to . . . make . . . amends!

"Amends" had been on Zack's vocabulary test the past week. That she had used that word meant she wanted to apologize by making up for her mistakes, compensating Zack for damages and injury.

Was that why she had also appeared at the Hanging Hill Playhouse over the summer?

To help him?

Maybe she'd stuffed her soul inside her sister's body and come all the way to North Chester to make amends but she never got the chance because the three aunts sent her packing.

Was his real mother a different person, like Grandpa Jim had said, now that she was dead and could look back on all the bad things she had done when she was alive?

Zack stared out the kitchen windows. The backyard was dark. A single yellow bug light glowed over the deck. Some leaves swirled in a corner behind the cold barbecue grill, which was covered up and ready to hibernate for the winter.

Tink, tink, tink.

A black-beaked bird was tapping, gently rapping at the patio door.

"Haw!" the bird croaked. "Haw-haw-haw!"

Its black eyes glistened like oil.

Weird as it seemed, Zack thought he recognized the

bird. Its laugh. Its cackle. It was the same raven that had been circling over the corn maze when he and Malik had gotten lost and bumped into the ghost of Mad Dog Murphy.

"Haw!"

"Grrrrr!"

Zipper jumped to the floor so he could snarl at the big black bird on the other side of the sliding glass door.

"Easy, Zip," said Zack. "He's outside. He can't hurt us."

When he said that, the bird lofted up off the deck, its massive wingspan blotting out the glow from the overhead porch light.

"Haw-haw-haw-haaaaw!"

Now the raven was laughing at Zack for thinking it couldn't hurt him.

The next morning, before first light, Jack the Lantern was back in Satan's saddle, his trusty guide bird perched on his bent arm.

"Take me to the boy!" he shouted as he tipped his elbow up to launch the raven.

The bird unfurled its wings and took flight, its midnight blackness nearly disappearing against the starry predawn sky.

The highwayman clicked his heels into his horse's flanks and Satan trotted toward the gates of Spratling Manor. Jack the Lantern threw back his head and laughed.

It was November 2.

The day Zachary Jennings would die.

93

Zack was still in bed but already wide awake when Judy came down to the basement at seven a.m.

"I sent Mrs. Emerson an email last night, after you guys went to bed," she said. "I asked her if she knew anything about this Jack the Lantern."

"What'd she find out?"

"Seems he was a notorious highwayman."

"Is that a toll collector or something?"

"No. A highwayman, back in olden days, was a thief who preyed on travelers. They'd attack stagecoaches or mail wagons. Some were like Robin Hood. They stole from the rich and gave to the poor."

"And Jack the Lantern?"

"Very un–Robin Hoodish. He dressed all in black and always wore a terrifying burlap mask with holes to make him look like a jack-o'-lantern."

"Is that how he got his name? Jack the Lantern?"

"Partially. He also used to toss firebombs in front of

carriages to spook the horses so he could stop a coach, slay the driver, steal the passengers' gold, and snatch baubles off the ladies."

Judy hesitated.

Zack knew that whatever she said next wasn't going to be good.

"Then he'd kidnap any children."

Zack's mouth went dry. "Why?"

"Well, if the families were wealthy, he'd ransom them back."

"And if they weren't so rich?"

"He'd sell the children as slave labor to factory owners and ship captains."

"And nobody knew Jack was really Barnabas Ickleby?"

"Nope. He fooled everybody for nearly three hundred years."

Suddenly, a horse whinnied out on the front lawn.

That was very bizarre.

Nobody in the neighborhood had a horse.

Aunt Ginny had woken up before anybody else in the house.

She knew that the most evil Ickleby of them all was now controlling the body of Norman Ickes and that Barnabas would soon come gunning for Zachary.

So Virginia Jennings, who had battled foul spirits and bullying demons all her life, would be prepared.

She quickly lit the jack-o'-lanterns lined up on the front porch railings, and then, very calmly, sat down in a rocking chair with another glowing pumpkin on her lap.

Moments later, the villain showed himself.

His glimmering black stallion pawed its hooves in the front lawn and snorted loudly. But it wouldn't move closer.

Not as long as the jack-o'-lanterns are lit. It can't. The illuminated gourds protect the house from all evil spirits, human or equine.

"Good morning, you wretched old woman!" shouted the rider with the hideously grinning face cut into his mask. "Where is the boy? Where is Zachary Jennings?"

A shiny black raven sat perched on the dark rider's shoulder like a villainous parrot.

"Why are you so interested in Zack, Norman?"

"Why do you call me that inglorious name when you now know who I truly am?"

"You mean Barnabas the leech?"

"Leech?"

"That's right. You're nothing but a freeloading, life-sucking parasite. A dybbuk clinging on to your distant relative's body because you're too chicken to move on to your eternal reward or, in your case, eternal punishment!"

"You dare call me a coward?"

"Yes, Norman. I just did."

"You shall pay for your words, you horrid hag."

"How?" Ginny held up the glowing pumpkin. "Are you and your horsey going to come up here and hurt me? Of course not. You're afraid of pumpkins, too!"

Hannah and Sophie came out on the porch.

"Oh, my," gasped Sophie. "Is that him?"

"Yes, dear," said Ginny in a tense stage whisper. "Did you bring the exorcism powders?"

Hannah was carrying Ginny's carpetbag. "It's all in here. For heaven's sake, sister, why do you taunt him?"

"It amuses me."

"Does he have the black heart stone?" asked Sophie.

"Aunt Ginny?" It was Zack. He and Judy were at the front door.

"Stay inside, dear. You too, Judy. We'll take care of this."

"I'm going to call the police," said Judy.

"No. Not yet. Soon that creature on the horse will be nothing more than a dazed and confused hardware-store clerk who will, hopefully, remember where they had him hide the black heart stone. Give us a minute."

"*One* minute," said Judy.

Ginny stood up from the rocking chair and turned her back to Jack the Lantern so she could consult with her two sisters.

"We shall initiate the exorcism."

"How?" asked Hannah.

"We can startle him with his false reflection from up here. I'll work the mirror. Hannah, you take the horn. Sophie, stand by with the powder. Once we have spiritual separation, we can sage Barnabas and begin the banishment incantation."

"I'll ask you one last time, ladies!" shouted Jack the Lantern. "Where is the boy? Where is young Zachary Jennings?"

Ginny twirled around.

"He's busy!"

"Doing what?"

"Getting ready for school!" shouted Sophie. "The bus will be coming along shortly to pick him up."

Jack tugged up on the reins. His black stallion pranced sideways. "Why, thank you, Sophia. How silly of me to forget. The big yellow carriage full of children that I have seen pass Haddam Hill so many times."

"Oops," peeped Sophie, putting her hand to her mouth. "I think I just made a boo-boo."

Jack pulled a pistol out of his belt, aimed it at Ginny.

"And just who do you think you're scaring with that, coward?" said Aunt Ginny defiantly.

"Your glowing gourds might stop *me* from coming up on that porch, sorceress, but they cannot stop my bullet!"

The raven perched on the masked man's shoulder squawked and flapped its wings.

Ginny reached into her carpetbag. Whipped out the stainless steel signal mirror.

Before she could use it, she heard a gun explode.

The pistol ball smacked Ginny hard.

The silvery mirror fell from her hand with a clatter.

Ginny felt a searing pain in her chest as the world began to spin.

"Oh, my," she squeaked.

And then she toppled to the floor.

25

As the old crone fell to her knees, Jack the Lantern threw back his head and cackled his lunatic laugh. Satan reared up on his hind legs and roared triumphantly.

"Away!" the masked highwayman cried. "Away!"

He tugged up on the reins hard. The horse wheeled right.

"Back to the crypt! Fly!"

He gave a swift kick, and with a jangle of stirrups, the horse broke into a full gallop.

Jack the Lantern would kidnap all the children crammed into the yellow carriage when it passed Haddam Hill.

He would demand a king's ransom for their safe return.

And once he had the money?

He would slay them all so none could bear witness against him.

But he would slay Zachary Jennings first!

Zack was kneeling on the porch, holding Aunt Ginny's hand.

"Don't worry, dear," she mumbled, a pained smile on her face. "It's only a flesh wound."

"The ambulance is on its way!" shouted Judy, who had called 911.

"Put this poultice on it," said Hannah, pressing a moist mass of cloth and herbs on the bloody bullet hole.

Aunt Ginny winced. "Ouch. Not so much pressure, dear."

"Hush," said Aunt Sophie. "Save your strength."

"Malik," mumbled Zack.

"What?" said Judy.

Zack motioned for his mom to join him where the aunts couldn't hear what they were talking about.

"What if, somehow, Jack the Lantern knows about the gold and the reward? What if Norman, somehow, told him? Malik will definitely be one of the kids he grabs first!"

"Run inside. You call Malik. I'll call your dad. Hurry!"

97

"Hello?"

"Malik?"

"Hi, Zack. Everything okay?"

"Don't go to school today."

"Why not?"

"Norman Ickes may be coming to get you."

"What?"

"Well, he's not really Norman right now."

"But . . ."

"Look, I gotta run. The ambulance is here."

"Ambulance?"

"Yeah. Norman just shot Aunt Ginny. I'll call you again when we're at the hospital. Bye."

Zack clicked off.

Malik stared at the phone.

Norman Ickes, his puzzle pal, had shot Zack's elderly aunt?

Malik turned on the early-morning TV news.

"This just in," said the reporter, "Norman Ickes strikes

again. Moments ago, the local hardware-store clerk, wanted for yesterday's robberies at Stansbury Stables and the Hi-Way 31 Eat and Run, appeared on horseback and shot an elderly woman who . . ."

Malik snapped off the TV.

Zack was right.

He needed to stay home from school today.

98

At Aunt Ginny's request, Zack and Judy rode in the back of the ambulance with her and the paramedic who had bandaged her shoulder wound.

A police car carrying Aunts Hannah and Sophie was right behind them.

"Do I look like a scuba diver, Zack?" asked Aunt Ginny, her voice weak. She had an oxygen tube stuck up her nostrils.

Zack smiled. "Sort of."

"Good. I always wanted to go scuba diving."

"Ma'am?" said the paramedic, who was holding her wrist, checking her pulse. "You need to take it easy, okay?"

"Yes, dear. Of course." Her voice was barely a whisper. "Judy?"

"Yes?"

"Take my purse." She gestured toward the bulging carpetbag.

"I'll keep an eye on it for you."

"No. You need to take my place."

"But . . ."

"The circle must number three, Judy. You, Sophie, and Hannah."

Judy nodded. She understood.

"Everything you need is in that bag."

Aunt Ginny was wheezing now.

"Zack?" He had to lean down to hear her.

"Yes, ma'am?"

"This is why I tricked you and your friends into opening the black heart stone: I knew that I, and my sisters, would one day die, that our confinement spell would then be broken. The Icklebys would escape. . . . I'm sorry . . . I . . ."

"Okay," said Judy, touching Zack on his back. "Let Ginny rest, hon."

Aunt Ginny closed her eyes.

Motion in the front of the ambulance caught Zack's attention.

Grandpa Jim! Sitting in the passenger seat.

"Shhh," he said. "Don't let on you can see and hear me. Ginny and Judy can't, because I don't want them to."

Zack budged his eyebrows up half a millimeter to ask Grandpa Jim what he was doing there.

"You've got to find that black heart stone, champ. You need to finish what Ginny started. Listen to what your mother told you."

Zack still had no idea what Grandpa Jim was talking about.

"Remember everything she said. *Everything!*"

"Zack?" It was Judy.

"Yeah?"

"You okay?"

"Yeah. I'm just worried about Aunt Ginny."

"She's very lucky," said the paramedic. "The bullet went clean through her shoulder."

Zack looked back to the front seat to check out Grandpa Jim's reaction to the good news.

Only he was gone.

Leaving Zack to wonder: What had his mother said that could help him find the stone?

Azalea Torres was on the school bus, cramming for a science test.

That meant opening the textbook for the first time, checking out the chapter.

"Got it," she muttered to herself. Yes, a photographic memory was a girl's best friend. Right now, she knew more about solar and geothermal energy than even Malik Sherman!

The bus made its standard fart noises, swung out its squeaky red stop sign, and came to a halt at the corner where Malik boarded.

Only he wasn't at the bus stop.

Three kids climbed aboard, but no Malik.

Maybe the big meeting of the Pettimore Trust down in New York City hadn't gone so well.

Losing his big reward, which was supposed to cover all his mom's medical bills, would be a total bummer. If that was what had happened, Azalea might need to go home sick today, too.

She'd ask Zack if he'd heard anything.

His stop was only two away.

Right after Haddam Hill and the totally creepy but totally cool cemetery.

100

Zack, Judy, Aunt Hannah, and Aunt Sophie sat in the emergency room waiting area.

It was nearly eight a.m.

A television suspended on a bracket was blaring the local news but nobody was paying much attention to it.

Judy was on her cell phone, talking with Zack's dad. He would be on the next train home to North Chester.

"Come straight to the hospital," Judy suggested. "Aunt Ginny will be here a while. . . . We will. . . . Love you, too."

Judy closed her cell and glanced up at the TV.

"What's that?"

She and Zack got up and walked closer to the monitor.

"That's Ickes and Son," said Zack. "The hardware store on Main Street."

The TV showed a short man, his face sad and gray, standing next to a big guy with a shaved head and a tiny chin beard. The big guy was chewing gum, grinning, and waving at the camera.

"That's Norman's father," said Zack. "And a Snertz who works at the hardware store."

As if to prove Zack correct, titles appeared on the bottom of the screen: Herman Ickes, father. Stephen Snertz, coworker.

The camera zoomed out and a reporter lady jabbed a microphone under Mr. Ickes's nose.

"This is terrible," he said. "I don't know what could have gotten into my son."

"The real question," said Zack, "is *who* got into his son."

"Didn't you recently fire your son?" asked the reporter.

"Yes."

"Didn't you have his name painted over on your sign?"

Stephen Snertz grabbed for the microphone. "It wasn't his name. It was the 'and Son.' Basically, Herman here was telling the world he no longer had a son, isn't that right, Herm?"

Mr. Ickes didn't answer. He dropped his head in shame.

So the reporter concentrated on Snertz.

"You worked with Norman. Do you think his father's recent actions are what sent the younger Mr. Ickes over the edge?"

"Definitely. Of course, Norman was always nuttier than squirrel poop."

"So you're not surprised at this turn of events?"

"Nah. Except the horse. Who knew the nerd could ride?"

The reporter turned to face the camera, which zoomed

out even further, taking in the hardware store and the other shops lining Main Street.

"There you have it, Chip," said the reporter. "A father's public humiliation of his only son sends him spiraling into a violent rampage that has terrorized a picture-perfect small town in this bucolic corner of Connecticut."

While she talked, the camera panned right and took in more storefronts, the village green and town hall, the town clock tower . . .

The clock tower!

With its hands rusted in place.

Where the time was always frozen at 9:52.

That was what his mother had told him right before she disappeared.

Nine-fifty-two!

She had broken the rules and told him exactly where he had to go.

"The town clock!" Zack said to Judy.

"What?"

"That's where they hid the black heart stone!"

101

Azalea was seated in her usual spot near the rear of the bus, so she saw him first.

A guy dressed all in black and wearing one of those hats they wear in Colonial Williamsburg came charging down the cemetery hill on a horse.

"Um, Ms. Tiedeman?" she called up to the bus driver.

The guy on the horse was gaining on them. Azalea could see he was wearing a mask that made his head look like a burlap pumpkin, complete with the triangle eyes and nose and the sawtooth jack-o'-lantern grin.

"Ms. Tiedeman?" She shouted it this time.

The bus driver looked up at her rearview mirror.

"What's the problem back there, Azalea?"

The horse rider raced past Azalea's window. He was moving faster than the bus. She heard him scream, "Onward, Satan! Fly, Satan, fly!"

Great. Pumpkin Head's horse was named Satan.

"I think this guy wants us to pull over."

The bus driver leaned forward to check her side-view mirror.

"Stand and deliver!" the horse rider shouted as he drew parallel to the driver's window.

"What?" said Ms. Tiedeman.

"Stand and deliver, I say!"

"Yeah? Well, I say, 'Shut up and go away!'"

"Pull over to the side of the road, wench!"

"Sorry, pal. I have a schedule to keep."

Azalea felt the rumbling bus accelerate.

"Everybody buckled up?" the bus driver shouted at the panoramic mirror, in which she could see all the kids. "Grab hold of a seat back and brace yourself!"

Then she pressed the pedal to the metal.

But the black stallion, with bubbly foam streaming out around its mouth bit, pumped it up a notch, too. The colonial jockey reached down into a saddlebag and pulled out a flaming lantern, which he hurled about twenty yards up the road.

It hit the asphalt and erupted into a gassy fireball.

"Hang on, kids!" Ms. Tiedeman pulled her steering wheel hard to the right and then immediately back to the left, sending the school bus careening through a cloud of smoke, but clear of the blaze.

Azalea turned around and saw that the bandit on horseback was behind the bus now, having just blown through the smoke cloud where the lantern grenade had exploded.

He spurred his horse hard, and in an instant, horse and rider were only a few feet away from the bus's rear bumper.

Being a soldier's daughter, Azalea leapt into action.

She raced to the back of the bus.

"Azalea?" shouted the bus driver. "Sit down! I'm pulling over."

"Not yet. I'll knock this dude on his butt." She reached the rear emergency exit. The masked man was right outside and standing up in his saddle.

Excellent!

Azalea would kick open the door and whack him off his pony.

She reached for the handle.

Pumpkin Head leapt up, grabbed hold of a light or something.

And hauled himself onto the roof of the bus!

102

Zack and Judy were whisked home in a police car.

"I'll go in and grab Zipper," said Zack as Judy transferred Aunt Ginny's carpetbag full of gear to her own sporty sedan. "We might need his nose to help us find where they hid the stone."

"Great idea. And call Malik. Tell him we'll swing by and pick him up."

"Right." .

They needed Malik to take the black stone puzzle apart again, which was the only way to dislodge the miniature black heart in the center. If Judy, Aunt Hannah, and Aunt Sophie could exorcise the Ickleby demon out of Norman's body and then crush the black core, Barnabas's soul would go straight down to H-E-double-hockey-sticks.

Zack called Malik.

"Can you take apart that black heart again?"

"Oh, yes. The second time you work a puzzle always takes much less time."

"Great. We'll meet you out front in five."

Next, Zack scooped up Zipper, who was taking his morning nap, and started to carry him out to the car.

"Time for your nose to wake up, boy. It's got work to do!"

Zipper barked once, leapt out of Zack's arms, and raced him out to Judy's car.

103

"Hop in!" Zack shouted to Malik.

Malik slid into the backseat with Zipper.

"Where are we going?" he asked as they pulled out of the driveway.

"The clock tower," said Zack. "Downtown. That's where they hid the black heart stone."

"Who?"

Zack didn't have time to explain the whole dybbuk, soul-in-a-body-that-wasn't-its-body deal. So he simplified things. "The bad guys."

"I see. And how do we know the clock tower is where the bad guys stashed their loot?"

"My mother told me."

"I did?" said Judy from behind the wheel.

"I meant my other mother."

"Excuse me? Zack?" said Malik, raising his hand.
"Yeah?"

"I thought your birth mother was dead."

"She is. But, well, she found a way to come back to life just so she could stop by the house and drop me a huge hint."

"I see. Well, that was very thoughtful of her."

"Yeah. I think being dead has made her a much better person."

As the bus eased to a stop, Azalea heard boot heels clomping along its riveted steel roof.

"You stupid bus driver," whined Kurt Snertz, an eighth grader who was sitting near the front of the bus today, just so he could finger-flick a new kid's ears. "Why'd you pull over?"

"Kurt?" said Azalea.

"What?"

"Be cool."

"Make me."

"You heard the lass," croaked the masked man as he strode onto the bus, both pistols aimed at Snertz. "Sit still, lad."

"Yes, sir," Kurt said, gulping. Azalea thought he might burst into tears.

"Children," said the masked man, "I hereby declare

you all to be my hostages!" His voice was hoarse and raspy. "May God have mercy on your souls!"

And then the bad guy's eyes went buggy as he cocked his head sideways as if he was listening to something nobody else could hear.

105

Norman Ickes was having a blast sharing his body with his evil ancestor Barnabas.

He'd punched people, gone horseback riding, killed a priest, and shot an old lady who'd been making fun of him.

Now he was in heaven. The smart-mouthed kid in the third row was Stephen Snertz's nephew—the punk who had crazy-glued Norman's fingers to the hardware store phone one Saturday when he came in to watch football with his uncle.

"*Barnabas!*" his soul cried out.

"*Silence,*" his dybbuk thought back. "*I am otherwise engaged.*"

"*That boy, the beefy one with the red hair.*"

"*What about him?*"

"*He is a Snertz.*"

"*So?*"

"*The Snertzes are the richest family in all of North Chester.*"

"*What about the Spratlings?*"

"*They're all dead. Besides, the Snertzes are richer. Mark my word, that boy will fetch us a handsome ransom.*"

"*Where are his people, that I might make my demands known?*"

"*Go see his uncle. Stephen Snertz.*"

"*And where might Stephen Snertz tarry at this hour?*"

"*The hardware store on Main Street!*"

"Coachwoman?" Norman heard Barnabas say to the bus driver. "Take me to the hardware store on Main Street, where I shall parley with the Snertz family for their heir's ransom! Satan, follow the yellow carriage!"

Checkmate, thought Norman. *We're comin' to get you, Stephen!*

106

"What *is* that school bus doing over near the hardware store?" asked Malik from the backseat. "Was there a field trip today?"

"I don't think so," said Zack, who thought a hardware store would be a pretty odd place to take a field trip.

"I don't remember signing any permission slips," added Judy.

She had parked her car right in front of the town clock tower, the tallest building in North Chester. Zack looked up at its face, five stories above the street.

Nine-fifty-two.

His dad used to joke that no matter what train he took to New York City in the morning, it was always the nine-fifty-two, because the town clock had been frozen in that position for as long as he could remember. Zack, of course, wished he had figured out his mother's clue sooner.

Next he checked out the door at the base.

It looked to be unlocked, because a stiff breeze squeaked it open a crack.

"Oh, no," said Judy, who was looking up the block to the town hall. "There's a black horse standing next to the bus."

"Unusual," said Malik. "You certainly don't see that every day."

Now it was Zack's turn to say, "Oh, no," because he was the first one to see Jack the Lantern climb off the bus, a pistol poked into Azalea Torres's back.

He was using her as a shield!

"Who's that guy in the mask manhandling Azalea?" asked Malik.

"Your friend," said Zack. "Norman Ickes."

107

"Where is Squire Stephen Snertz?" Azalea heard the masked man snarl at the crowd outside the hardware store.

In the mob were a bunch of TV reporters with microphones and cameras. They swung around to aim their gear at the shaved-head goon who had harassed Norman Ickes on Halloween night—the dude who had pulled the plug on all the pumpkins.

In the distance, Azalea could hear the wail of police sirens.

"What is going on?" the masked man whispered tensely. "What is making that high-pitched squeal? Why are all these townsfolk idling about? I am Jack the Lantern. I lurk in the shadows, where none can find me. . . ."

"Sorry, sir," said Azalea. "Somebody must've alerted the authorities."

"The king's soldiers are coming?"

"Uh, no. The police."

The masked man pulled her closer to his chest.

Great. To shoot him, the cops would have to try to miss her.

"Where is Stephen Snertz?" the guy who called himself Jack shouted again. This time, he brandished a new weapon: a very modern, very lethal-looking pistol.

Azalea was eager to hurry things along.

"That's him. The bald dude with the chin goatee."

Stephen Snertz brought his hand up to his chin, trying to hide his facial hair.

"Sir Snertz," said the kidnapper, "know that I hold your scion as my hostage!"

"M-m-my w-w-what?" said Snertz, who was trembling pretty bad and looked like he might wet himself.

"He means your nephew," said Azalea. "Kurt? He's on the bus."

Stephen Snertz sort of squirmed and snorted some snot up his schnozz before he said, "So?"

"We two must come to terms," said the man in the mask.

"About w-w-what?"

"Young Kurt's ransom!"

"R-r-ransom? What are you talking about, Norman?"

"My name is Jack the Lantern!"

Snertz put a hand on his hip and tried to look tough.

"Really? I thought it was Crazy Izzy Ickleby."

"That was yesterday. This is today."

"Man," Snertz chortled, "you are nuttier than all the pecan pies in Georgia!"

Azalea heard a pistol hammer cock back right next to her ear.

"Hey! Th-th-that's my pistol!" said Snertz.

"Indeed it is!" said the masked man. Then he started mumbling to himself. "No, Norman. Not yet." He cleared his throat and loudly addressed Snertz again: "If, sir, you do not meet my demands and present me with twenty pounds of solid gold bullion within the hour, I shall be forced to sell young Master Snertz to certain ship captains I know of in these parts."

Azalea raised an eyebrow. Pumpkin Head was definitely living in the past. There hadn't been any ship captains living in North Chester since the nineteenth century.

"Drop your weapons!" cried a brusque voice through a bullhorn.

Azalea looked left. Sheriff Hargrove and six of his deputies had their guns up and aimed at Pumpkin Head, which meant they were also, more or less, aimed at her.

100

"Is the door locked?" asked Judy, studying the base of the clock tower.

"No," said Zack. "Somebody busted it open."

"Probably Norman," said Malik. "He's the top lock picker in our puzzle club."

"Hurry, guys," said Judy. "Find the stone. Toss it in Aunt Ginny's bag with the rest of the junk."

Zack grabbed the carpetbag from Malik in the backseat.

"I'll see what's going on with the school bus. When you find the black heart, use the signal mirror. Flash it at me from down here in the doorway," said Judy.

"We will," said Zack, yanking up his door handle.

"I'll call Hannah and Sophie; they have Aunt Ginny's cell phone."

"But wait—they don't have a car."

"They can take a taxi."

Zack nodded. He had seen some waiting in the hospital parking lot.

"Okay. Go. And, Malik?" Judy said.

"Yes, ma'am?"

"Set a new world record tearing it apart, okay?"

"Will do, Mrs. Jennings!"

"Come on!" said Zack.

He, Malik, and Zipper headed into the clock tower while Judy jogged across the street and up the block to the bus.

The crowd grew larger behind the hastily erected police barriers on Main Street.

Judy saw Scot Smith, the principal of the middle school; Sheriff Ben Hargrove and half the North Chester Police Department; Mr. Ickes and the gum-cracking hardware store employee from TV, Stephen Snertz; not to mention all sorts of TV camera crews, which kept piling out of vans with satellite dishes on their roofs.

Jack the Lantern was back on the bus with Azalea and the other schoolchildren, several of whom Judy could hear sobbing through the windows.

A police officer carefully tried to approach the horse and got a nasty kick for his trouble.

"He has guns!" Judy heard someone say behind her.

"Is it really Norman Ickes?" asked another.

"What's with that mask? He looks like a jack-o'-lantern."

"You mean a jackass!" shouted Stephen Snertz very

bravely, because the police had their weapons trained toward the bus. Snertz stood with a small group in front of the hardware store. "Who does he think he is, anyway? Saying he wants me to ransom my stupid nephew?" Now he gave Mr. Ickes, Norman's father, a quick shove. "I told you: Your son is nuttier than squirrel poop!"

Judy pulled out her cell phone and hit the speed dial number she had programmed to ring Aunt Ginny's cell phone.

"Yes? Hello?"

"Aunt Sophie, the dybbuk is here on Main Street. He's hijacked a busload of children!"

"Jack the Lantern strikes again, eh?"

"We three are needed. Immediately, if not sooner."

"Has Zack found the black heart stone?"

"Not yet. But he will."

"Wonderful. Ginny is in the recovery room. Hannah and I are on our way. She's outside, organizing transportation. It's time we sent the first and last of these Ickleby demons straight home to hell!"

After quickly sniffing the ground floor of the clock tower, Zipper charged up the spiral staircase.

Cheesy feet.

He smelled what he had smelled on Halloween night.

Every step smelled like cheesy feet.

Senses fully engaged, the dog zipped up five stories, round and round, to the top of the clock tower.

Zack and Malik were huffing and puffing behind him.

The two boys were breathing hard through their mouths.

That meant they weren't using their snouts so they didn't have to smell the stinky sock odor that oozed out of the hardware-store man's shoes with every step he took.

That was a good thing.

Very good.

Because smelling this much funky foot cheese was a job best fit for a dog!

111

Charging up the spiral staircase after Zipper, Zack and Malik finally entered the clockwork room, a chamber on the fifth floor with a ceiling at least fifteen feet tall.

One whole wall was the back side of the massive clock face. Now that they were inside, Zack could see three or four places where chunks of the milky white glass had been broken out. Dusty shafts of sunlight shot through the holes, casting bright circles on the opposite wall.

"Fascinating," said Malik. "I've never been inside a clock before."

"Me neither," said Zack.

There was a ten-foot-square wooden deck in the middle of the crowded room, its oak planks stained with globs of grease and machine oil. A series of toothy gears, spiraling springs, and cogwheels—each one larger than the one before it—climbed up to the cranks and axles that once turned the clock hands.

"Okay," said Zack. "If you wanted to hide the stone puzzle, where would you put it?"

"Someplace high," said Malik. "You could scale those gear teeth and prop it on a ledge or on top of an idle crankshaft."

Zipper barked once. His nose was still glued to the floor, the way it had been all the way up the steps. Now he sniffed a straight line across the wooden deck and came to a large lead weight tied to a thick rope.

"You think he smells Norman's scent?" asked Malik.

"Yes! That's why he ran up the staircase so fast!"

Zip went up on his hind legs and barked at the rafters, where the rope looped over a pulley.

Great.

Zack Jennings, who had flunked every phys ed test he had ever taken, would need to shinny up a rope to see if Zipper was right.

"Wish me luck," he said to Malik.

Zack knew he was the one who had to do the rope climb.

Because Malik Sherman was the only kid at Pettimore Middle School who had flunked more P.E. tests than he had.

112

The rope was tied to a bell-shaped lead weight, part of the old clock's winding mechanism, similar to the chained brass pinecones that drove his grandfather's cuckoo clock.

Zack grabbed the cord with both hands above his head. Pulling down on the rope while jumping, he lifted himself into the air. He quickly used his feet to pinch the rope and anchor himself in position.

Now he reached as high as he could with his arms and gripped the rope tightly so he could release his feet and, crunching his stomach muscles, bring his knees to his chest and once again snag the rope between his feet.

"How'd you do that?" asked Malik.

"Coach Mike taught me."

Now he just had to do it five or six more times.

And not look down.

Looking down always made him realize what he was actually doing, and then he couldn't do it anymore.

Grunting, groaning, grabbing, and gripping, he finally made it up to the pulley.

"Is it there?" Malik shouted from below.

"Hang on."

Now Zack had to try something he'd never trained for: While holding on to the rope with one hand and squeezing his feet hard, he reached up and felt around on the top of the grimy crossbeam the pulley was bolted to.

He felt nothing but splinters.

So he slid his hand the other way.

And knocked something off the ledge!

"Got it!" shouted Malik.

Zack looked down.

His friend had made a perfect two-handed breadbasket catch.

Zipper barked and wagged his tail.

"Is it the black heart stone?" Zack shouted.

"Yep! Come on down."

Zack slid down the rope.

Exactly the way his gym teacher, Coach Mike, had told him *not* to.

He had nasty rope burns on his palms and knees but he didn't care. Malik was already twisting and turning the black heart stone and taking it apart!

"I need to find the signal mirror," said Zack, rummaging through Aunt Ginny's bag. "It's time to call in the herbologists!"

He found the silvery square and ran over to the clock face.

There was a broken-out spot about two feet off the floor, between the V and the VI.

He knelt down to flash Judy the signal.

He could see her near the school bus, shielding her eyes with one hand, staring at the base of the tower.

He tilted the mirror back and forth a couple of times, bounced Judy a sunbeam.

She blinked. Looked up. Waved.

A raven cawed.

"Haw-haw-haw."

Zack stuck his head through the hole.

The big black bird was perched on the frozen minute hand.

It ruffled out its giant wings and took off—flying straight for the big yellow bus!

113

Azalea stared at the muzzle of the pistol the masked maniac had pointed at her nose.

"Where have all these people come from?" he asked.

"Well, these days, when there's, like, a disaster, word spreads fast. Text messages, tweets . . ."

Jack the Lantern shook his head. His eyeballs were looking crazier and crazier.

And the nut job had three weapons: two old-fashioned pirate pistols, one very modern revolver.

"This is not how I had planned it to be! I am out-numbered. Out-armed. I must act boldly! Where is Zachary Jennings? Why is he not on this carriage?"

"I think he took a sick day," said Azalea.

Suddenly, glass shattered.

A giant black bird busted through the rear window of the bus and swooped up the center aisle. It landed on a seat back and started croaking and cawing like crazy. Glass chips tinkled out of its feathers.

Pumpkin Head tilted his head sideways and started nodding—like he understood everything the crow creaked out.

"But did he find the black heart stone?" he snapped.

"Haw!"

"Curses!" Pumpkin Head balled up his fist and shook it at the bus's ceiling. "Why must this Jennings family torment me through the ages?"

Furious, he clutched Azalea's arm and dragged her up the aisle to the back door of the bus.

When the police raised their pistols and rifles in response, the masked man jammed one of his pistols into Azalea's ear.

"Satan! Come hither!" he shouted out the broken window as he kicked the door open.

As the black steed approached the door, the crazed bandit called to the crowd, "Shoot me, and she dies."

Now, keeping his back to the school bus and never lowering his pistol, Jack lifted Azalea into his arms and leapt into the horse's saddle, holding the girl in front of him.

"Come, lass. You and I are going across the street to visit with your friend."

Malik *seemed* to be having a hard time taking the black heart apart.

Zack and Zipper were both watching every move he made. Even the ones that didn't seem to work. Pieces weren't coming out of the puzzle at the same pace they had when Malik tore the thing apart the first time.

"Everything okay?"

"Zack?"

"Yeah?"

"I don't perform well under pressure."

"Right," said Zack, backing up toward the clock face. "So me and Zip will just wait over here. Give us a holler when you've got the black heart core. We'll just be waiting. . . ."

"Zack?"

"Yeah?"

"You're pressuring me again!"

"Sorry."

Malik swiped some sweat out of his eyes.

Zack figured he'd better not say anything else.

So he peeked through the hole in the glass and checked out the action over by the school bus.

He wished he hadn't.

Jack the Lantern was leaping from the back of the bus onto the black horse, using Azalea as his human shield!

115

"Watch out!" Judy screamed.

Aunts Sophie and Hannah were just about to climb out of a taxi when the black stallion came charging around the bus.

Jack the Lantern had Azalea Torres in front of him on the saddle, so even though all the cops had their weapons trained on him, no one dared shoot at the moving target, for fear they'd accidentally hit the girl.

"Look at him!" shouted Stephen Snertz. "Hiding behind a girl! I told you—the guy's a wuss!"

Suddenly, Jack pulled up on the reins and wheeled his snorting horse to the right. The stallion made a sharply angled turn, mirroring the move a knight makes in chess.

"Oh, crap!" screamed Stephen Snertz when he realized that the masked demon had an arm over Azalea's shoulder. In his hand was a pistol aimed straight at the hardware-store clerk.

Snertz turned and made a mad dash for the door.

He almost made it, too.

But Jack the Lantern let loose with a cannon blast from his raised pistol.

The bullet smacked Snertz in the butt and sent him sailing forward through the hardware-store window. Glass shattered and Snertz landed with a belly flop on all the carved jack-o'-lanterns in the window display, many of which were already wilting after sitting in the sun so long. When the mounted maniac saw Snertz sprawled out in the rotting pumpkin patch, he started laughing insanely. All the police officers lowered their weapons an inch or two to marvel at his madness.

"Away, Satan! Fly like the wind!"

With a snick of his tongue and a click of his heels, Jack was once again racing away from the school bus and the hardware store.

"He's heading for the clock tower!" someone shouted.

"Get the kids off the bus!" yelled the sheriff.

Azalea Torres was Jack's only remaining hostage.

A pair of police officers dashed up the street after him while Sheriff Hargrove and his deputies secured the other children.

Jack leapt from his horse and yanked Azalea out of the saddle. With his modern-looking pistol aimed at her head, they backed toward the doorway of the clock tower.

"My son and Malik Sherman are in there!" Judy shouted to the police.

"Keep away, fools!" cried Jack the Lantern. "If any of you dare come in after me, this young lass dies!"

Judy watched as the demon pulled Azalea into the dark tower and slammed the door shut.

Now Jack the Lantern held three children hostage: Azalea, Malik, and Zack!

116

"Got it!" said Malik.

Zack pulled back from his peephole.

"He's coming!"

"Who?"

"Jack the Lantern."

"You mean Norman?"

"Yeah."

From down below, they heard a heavy steel beam thudding into a bracket. The door was barred. The police wouldn't be able to storm the tower and rescue them.

"He's got Azalea," said Zack.

"Move," they heard a scratchy voice cry at the bottom of the spiral staircase.

"Let go of my arm already," growled Azalea.

Zack, Malik, and Zipper knelt at the top of the spiral staircase, straining to hear every word echoing up from five stories below.

"Climb the stairs, missy. I need to parley with Mr. Jennings. He has something I desire."

Zack heard the unmistakable sharp click of a pistol hammer being cocked.

"We're up here!" he shouted down the steps. "And if you hurt Azalea, I'm going to toss this stupid stone down to my aunts, who just showed up and know what to do with it!"

"Zack?" Azalea shouted.

"Yeah?"

"Pumpkin Head put away his pistol."

Good.

"My name is Jack the Lantern!"

"Fine. Whatever."

Azalea never lost her cool. Zack just hoped she hadn't lost that photographic memory she was always bragging about, either.

"We're coming up," Zack heard her say. "Let. Go. Of. My. Arm!"

Now all Zack heard was the heavy *thunk-thunk-thunk* of boot heels against steel stairs.

"It's up to us," he whispered to Malik. "We three must agree."

"About what?"

"Smashing Barnabas Ickleby's tiny black heart!"

117

"They're on the second floor," said Malik, who was still perched at the top of the spiral staircase, counting boot clicks while Zack rummaged through Aunt Ginny's bag.

"Okay. I think I've got everything we need." He jammed the signal mirror and party horn into his back pockets. Wadded up the exorcism words into a paper ball. "Malik?"

"Yeah?"

"You're gonna be our powder man."

"Huh?"

Zack handed Malik a glass jar. "Extract of Newt Eye & Cow Hoof" was scribbled on its lid.

"Wait for your cue, then sidearm the whole jar at him." Zack unscrewed the cap.

"The powder will fly out."

"That's the idea. Stand over there. Near those gears. Zip? You stick with me."

The thunk of the boots became louder. Jack and Azalea were coming closer.

"Zack?" said Malik.

"Yeah?"

"What exactly are we doing here?"

Zack smiled and shot Malik a wink. "We're about to become amateur herbologists."

118

Azalea's head bobbed up in the stairwell first.

Zack tossed her the paper wad.

She caught it. Gave him a puzzled look.

Zack did some rapid-fire hand signals he hoped she understood.

Azalea nodded. She quickly unfolded the sheet and read it.

Her eyes bugged out, but she took it all in. Half a second later, she crumpled the paper back up into a ball.

Now the man in the mask appeared.

"Greetings, Zachary."

Zack just nodded.

"Where is it, boy?"

Now Zack held open his right hand. The miniature black heart from the center of the stone was nestled in his palm. "You mean this?"

"Give it to me!"

Zack retreated half a step. "No way."

"What? You dare refuse me?"

Zack retreated another half step.

"I need that black heart."

Zack took another backward step.

Jack the Lantern shoved Azalea aside. Held out his hand. "Give it to me, boy!"

Zack took one last giant step backward.

And was standing directly in the spot hit by the sunbeam streaming through the biggest broken-out hole in the clock face.

He whipped up the signal mirror with his free hand.

A blinding shaft of light streaked across the room and seared a rectangle of white over Jack the Lantern's triangle eyeholes.

The masked man froze in his tracks.

"Azalea?" shouted Zack. "You're on!"

"We three declare it so, the uninvited visitor must now go," said Azalea with a shrug, because, Zack could tell, she had no idea why she had committed such nonsense to memory.

But she kept on going. "Thrice the brinded cat hath mew'd."

Since they didn't have a cat, Zack gave Zipper the hand command for "Speak."

Zip howled.

Zack tucked the tiny black heart into his shirt pocket and motioned for Malik to move closer, for Azalea to take a step to her left.

The three friends were forming a circle around the frozen highwayman.

"Round the dybbuk now we go," chanted Azalea, doing the whole thing from memory. "Leave this body by the toe. Spirit, under cold stone lie; you have had your chance to die."

"Sprinkle the powder," Zack said to Malik, who flung the whole sparkling contents of his open jar at the back of the bandit's head. Glittery clumps landed in the gullies on all three sides of his hat.

Zack stretched out his hands. Malik and Azalea understood. They linked hands with Zack and each other and started circling Jack the Lantern, ring-around-the-rosy style.

"Eye of newt and hoof of cow," Azalea said dramatically, nearing her big finish. "Leave this body, leave it now!"

Zack pulled out the tiny tin party horn and blew sour trumpet blasts like it was a World Cup soccer match.

"Is that really necessary?" asked Azalea, scrunching up her shoulders in an attempt to cover her ears.

"Yeah. The sour notes jar the soul out of the body."

"Look!" said Malik.

Jack the Lantern started to quiver.

And shimmy.

And shake.

His body slumped to the floor.

A purple mist seeped up out of his crumpled form.

The violet cloud quickly took shape.

The ghost of Barnabas Ickleby rose beside the body of Norman Ickes.

120

"I need a hammer or something!" Zack shouted.

He'd forgotten to look for one in the carpetbag.

"Foolish children," snarled the demonic ghost.

Zack raced back to the bag.

"You have done nothing but set my spirit free from this mortal coil. I shall return again—in a new body, a stronger body. I have other descendants. I shall find them."

Maybe you will, Zack thought, because he couldn't find anything to whack the stone with.

"And when I do, you three shall pay for what you tried to do to me."

Zack at least found a sage candle!

He sparked the tip.

Tossed it at Ickleby's feet.

"What?" The ghost laughed. "You cannot stun me into submission. My spirit is far too strong for such tricks. Don't waste your sage, boy!"

"What's going on, Zack?" asked Azalea. "Why are you tossing road flares around the room?"

"There's probably a ghost in here, right, Zack?" said Malik.

"Yeah. The spirit that possessed Norman Ickes."

"For real?" said Azalea. "Where is he?"

"Probably in the smoke," said Malik.

"No. Way!" Azalea fanned the air. Tried to see the spirit. Couldn't.

Zipper nudged Zack in the back with his snout.

"Not now, boy." Zack was pulling everything out of the carpetbag. The sage didn't immobilize Barnabas the way it had the other Icklebys.

Maybe the demon was right.

Maybe his spirit was too twisted for the sage to touch it.

Zack tore through the bag in a flurry. He tossed out a spice jar, a bundle of dried herbs tied with twine, more candles, a roll of breath mints, a pair of tongs—everything except what he needed.

Zipper nudged him harder.

Zack whipped around. "What is it, Zip?"

His trusty dog held something in his mouth like a bone.

A rock hammer!

"Good boy! You guys?"

Malik and Azalea crouched down to join Zack around the small black heart. While Ickleby ranted and Zipper snarled, Zack quickly consulted with his two friends.

"Shall we three send this soul straight to the underworld?" asked Zack.

"Yeah!" said Malik.

"Whatever," said Azalea.

"We three agree?" asked Zack.

And all three friends said it together: "We three agree!"

Zack smashed the hammer down hard.

The tiny black heart exploded with a sharp bang like he had smacked a roll of cap gun caps. Then it burst into a puff of violet smoke, which vanished in a flash of purple light.

The room was quiet.

Until, behind them, Norman Ickes began to moan.

121

Judy heard a small explosion, like a firecracker.

Or another pistol shot!

The crowd gathered around the base of the clock tower looked up in horror.

The big black horse bolted free from the distracted police officer holding its reins and trotted up Main Street.

A black raven circled overhead, like a vulture hungry for carrion it could peck to pieces.

And then Zack stuck his head out the hole in the clock, waving Jack the Lantern's tricornered hat.

"We're okay. Norman just surrendered."

The crowd cheered!

"What was that noise, Zachary?" shouted Aunt Hannah.

"His heart breaking!" shouted Zack. Aunt Hannah, Aunt Sophie, and Judy smiled. They knew what Zack meant.

"You sure you're okay, Zack?" shouted Sheriff Hargrove.

"Yeah. We're all fine."

"You kids did good, Zack."

"Thank you, sir."

"Hang tight up there. We're coming in." The sheriff turned to two of his deputies. "Go grab the battering ram. We're breaking down that darn door!"

122

Norman Ickes stumbled to his feet.

His legs were a little wobbly.

"What happened? Where am I?"

"We're in the top of the town clock tower," said Zack. "The police should be up here soon."

"They're going to arrest me, aren't they?"

Malik and Azalea both looked at Zack.

"Maybe," said Zack. "See, some pretty strange stuff happened."

Norman made his way toward the clock face.

"Take it easy," suggested Azalea. "You'll probably feel a little dizzy for a while. I know I did after I got possessed."

"A ghost took you out for a joyride, Norman," added Malik.

"My dad's a lawyer," said Zack. "I think he can help you. Maybe you can plead temporary insanity or something."

Norman peered through a hole in the clock face.

"My father is down there. And Stephen Snertz is still alive? Why is everybody helping him into that ambulance?"

"I'm not really sure," said Zack. "You see, Malik and I—"

"I hate my father," said Norman, who wasn't really listening to anything Zack said. "He's a weakling. And that Snertz? He's a bully."

"I know. They all are. But like I was saying, my dad—"

"I should've killed them both," said Norman, "when I had the chance!"

"Excuse me?" said Malik.

"I liked being evil, Malik! You would, too! Having the rage of my wicked ancestors burning inside my body. I felt strong. Nobody could stop me. Not that Stephen Snertz, that's for sure. Why did you three take that away from me?"

"You were possessed by an evil spirit," said Zack, trying to explain.

"I wasn't possessed," said Norman. "I was fulfilled! I invited the demon into my body to make me the man I always dreamed I could be. And now I'm just Norman Ickes again?"

"You're a good guy," said Malik.

"A good guy?" He spat out the words. "A good guy. You mean a nerd and a geek. I don't want to live like that again."

"Take it easy," said Zack.

"You ruined me!"

"No, we . . ."

Norman didn't listen.

He turned to the giant clock face and pounded the glass with both balled-up fists.

The whole clock face crackled like thin ice and fell out of its frame in sheets of angled glass.

All that was left were the black scrolled hands.

"Stand and deliver!" Norman shouted to the crowd below, sweeping his arms out wide. "I am Jack the Lantern!"

A diving raven swooped past the wide-open circle that used to be a clock.

And Norman Ickes leapt from his perch to soar after it.

123

The next weekend, Zack, Azalea, and Malik went to Norman Ickes's funeral.

Stephen Snertz did not make it. He was in traction at the hospital, suspended upside down with his fractured fanny in a plaster cast.

Ebony, the black stallion possessed by Satan, had been captured near Spratling Manor and taken back to Stansbury Stables, where he was spending the weekend under the watchful eye of an expert animal psychologist.

At the funeral services, Norman's father announced that his son's coffin would not be buried in the Ickleby family crypt or anywhere near the Haddam Hill Cemetery.

"The cycle of evil and violence that has plagued my family all these years must stop," he told the mourners. "It must end with my son."

Zack totally agreed.

* * *

On Sunday afternoon, Zack and his dad drove the three aunts and their cats to the airport for their return flight to Florida while Judy stayed at home with Zipper, who almost wagged his tail off saying "buh-bye" to his departing kitty kin.

Aunt Ginny was bandaged but recovering nicely from her gunshot wound.

Thanks to Aunt Sophie's wide load, Aunt Ginny and Zack were, once again, scrunched up together in the backseat of the family van.

"You did good, Zack," Aunt Ginny said, patting him on the knee.

"Thanks. You too."

"Oh, dear."

"What's wrong?"

"We forgot to go to the Hedge Pig Emporium and order you that chocolate milk shake."

"That's okay, Aunt Ginny. Maybe next time you come visit."

"Are you sure? Because we can change our flight. Fly back tomorrow."

"Aunt Ginny, can I ask you a question?"

"Certainly."

"Is the chocolate milk shake only on the kids' menu?"

"What do you mean?"

"Would it work on you? Could you drink one and stop seeing ghosts?"

"What? And miss out on all the fun?"

"I'm serious."

Aunt Ginny sighed and thought about her answer. "Yes, Zack. I could. But I won't."

"Why not?"

"Well, dear, I think that those of us who can see and stop evil need to protect those who cannot."

"Yeah. That's kind of what I think, too."

"I know." She winked at him. "It runs in the family."

THANK YOU...

In my school visits, I have fun improvising a ghost story based on suggestions from the assembled students to teach about story structure, protagonists, and antagonists. So I am eternally grateful to the fifth grader who, when prompted for a good name for a bad guy, shouted out, "Ickleby!"

I'd also like to thank all those who made generous contributions to the Artemis Project animal rescue group in New York for a chance to name one of the aunts' cats. Pyewacket, Mister Cookiepants, and Mystic were the winners, along with all the strays the Artemis Project helps here in New York City.

Thank you also to R. Schuyler Hooke, the best editor on this metaphysical plane or any other; Nicole de las Heras, who makes my many-chaptered books look so good; Scott Altmann, who has made the last three covers so creepy; Lisa McClatchy from Kids @ Random House, who helps me organize all my school visits; Emily Pourciau, who tells the world about Zack and Judy; the copy editors, who have taught me things about colons I never realized; and everybody else at Random House Children's Books, who has been so terrific to me and my stories.

Thanks as always to my agent, Eric R. Myers, who in six short years has shepherded seventeen of my stories to publication.

And to all the teachers, students, librarians, and parents who have told other teachers, students, librarians, and parents about the Haunted Mystery series.

Finally, all the cats in the book would like to thank Jeanette, Parker, and Tiger Lilly—the three cats who allow me to share their office space when I write.

CHRIS GRABENSTEIN'S first three books for younger readers—*The Crossroads, The Hanging Hill,* and *The Smoky Corridor*—have won a bunch of accolades and awards, including two Agathas and one Anthony.

Born in Buffalo, New York (where sometimes it snows on Halloween), and raised in Tennessee (which is why Davy talks the way he does), Chris moved to New York City many years ago to become an actor and a writer. He did improvisational comedy in a Greenwich Village basement with some of the city's funniest performers, including this one guy named Bruce Willis. He used to write TV and radio commercials, cowrote the made-for-TV movie *The Christmas Gift,* starring John Denver, and even wrote for the Muppets.

Chris is also a *New York Times* bestselling author of such award-winning mysteries and thrillers for adults as *Tilt-A-Whirl, Rolling Thunder,* and *Slay Ride.*

Chris and his wife, the actress J. J. Myers, live in New York City with three cats and a dog named Fred, who has the best credits in the family: Fred starred on Broadway in *Chitty Chitty Bang Bang.* You can visit Chris (plus Fred and the cats) at ChrisGrabenstein.com. Chris loves hearing from readers. His email address is author@ChrisGrabenstein.com.